HOLD ON TO ME

SIERRA CARTWRIGHT

HAWKEYE

HOLD ON TO ME

Copyright @ 2021 Sierra Cartwright

First E-book Publication: January 2021

Editing by Nicki Richards, What's Your Story Editorial Services

Line Editing by Jennifer Barker

Proofing by Bev Albin, Cassie Hess-Dean, and ELF

Layout Design by Once Upon An Alpha, Shannon Hunt

Cover Design by Once Upon An Alpha, Shannon Hunt

Promotion by Once Upon An Alpha, Shannon Hunt

All rights reserved. Except for use in a review, no part of this publication may be reproduced, distributed, or transmitted in any form, or by any means, electronic or mechanical, including photocopying, recording, or by any information storage and retrieval system, without prior written permission of the author.

This is a work of fiction. Names, characters, places, brands, media, and incidents are either the products of the author's imagination or are used fictitiously, and any resemblance to any actual persons, living or dead, is entirely coincidental.

The author acknowledges the trademarked status and trademark owners of various products referenced in this work of fiction. The publication/use of these trademarks is not authorized, associated with, or sponsored by the trademark owners.

Adult Reading Material

Disclaimer: This work of fiction is for mature (18+) audiences only and contains strong sexual content and situations.

It is a standalone with my guarantee of satisfying happily ever after.

All rights reserved.

DEDICATION

For all the wonderful people in my life who make this possible. Angie, Bev, Cassie, Jennifer, Miss Whit, Nicki, Shannon. Your support means more than you will ever know.

Especially for ELF. I appreciate you.

I'd like to give a special shoutout to Linda Pantlin Dunn. You brighten the world every single day.

To my review team—you totally rock my socks! Thank you!

To all members of the Super Stars—you're simply the best.

Newsletter subscribers—I see you out there!

And mostly, if you're reading this book, the dedication is to you. Every time I sit down at my computer, I think of you, and I thank you for letting me be part of your life. I am grateful for your notes, kind words, interactions on social media. I appreciate you and value you.

CHAPTER ONE

HAWKEYE

"No fucking way, Hawkeye." In case that wasn't clear enough, Jacob Walker tipped back the brim of his cowboy hat and leveled a stare at his friend and former commander across the small, rickety table that separated them.

The stench of cheap whiskey and loneliness hung in the air—as putrid as it was familiar.

Through the years, they'd held dozens of meetings at this kind of place. Didn't matter which fucked-up hellhole they were in—Central America, the Middle East, Texas, or here, a small, all but forgotten Colorado mountain town, a place with no security cameras, where neither of them were known.

As usual, Hawkeye dressed to blend in with the locals—jeans, scuffed boots, and a heavyweight canvas jacket that could be found on almost every ranch in the state. He'd added a baseball cap with a logo of a tractor company embroidered on the front. Today, he also wore a beard. No doubt it would be gone within an hour of his walking back outside into the crisp, clean air.

At one time, Jacob thrived on clandestine meetings. The anticipation alone was enough to feed adrenaline into his veins, and he lived for the vicarious thrill.

But life was different now.

After a final, fateful job in Colombia that left an American businessman's daughter dead, Jacob walked away from Hawkeye Security.

He returned to the family ranch and a world he no longer recognized. His grandfather had died, no doubt from the stress of managing the holdings by himself. Though Jacob's grandmother never uttered a critical word, he knew she was disappointed that he'd missed the funeral. He wasn't even in the same country when he was needed the most.

When she passed, he stood alone at the graveside, the only family mourner, like she'd no doubt been a few years before.

Spurred by equal measures of guilt and regret, he poured himself into managing the family's holdings as a way to redeem himself. Then, because of his loneliness and the horrible dreams after Colombia, he did it as a way to save himself.

"The op will take less than a month." Hawkeye shrugged. "Give or take. I'll give you three of our best agents—Johnson, Laurents, Mansfield. You can man the gate, rather than just utilizing the speaker box. Another on perimeter. One for relief. You have the space and a bunkhouse."

Jacob shook his head to clear it of the ever-present memories. "Is there a part of my refusal that you don't understand?" Of course there was. When Hawkeye wanted something, nothing would dissuade him. That willful determination had made him a force on the battlefield as well as in the business arena. "When I quit, I meant it." He took a swig from his longneck beer bottle. "No regrets." The words were mostly true. There were times he wanted the camaraderie and wanted to flex his brain as well as his muscles. There was also the sweet thrill of the hunt. And making things right in the world.

Rather than argue, Hawkeye removed his cap long enough for Jacob to get a look at his former boss. Worry lines were trenched between his eyebrows. In all his years, Jacob had never seen dark despair in those eyes. "Yesterday, Inamorata received what appeared to be a birthday card from her sister."

Ms. Inamorata was Hawkeye's right-hand woman and known for her ability to remain calm under duress. She could be counted on to deal with local and federal authorities, smoothing over all the details. Rather seriously, Hawkeye said she batted cleanup better than any major leaguer.

Jacob told himself to stand up, thank Hawkeye for the drink, then get the hell out of here while he still could. Instead, he remained where he was.

"There was a white powder inside."

Jesus. "Anthrax?"

"Being tested. She took appropriate precautions and received immediate medical assistance. Antibiotics were prescribed as a precaution." Hawkeye paused. "There were no warning signs that the piece of mail was suspicious."

Meaning the postmark matched the return address. The postage amount was correct, and there was nothing protruding from the envelope.

Jacob knew Inamorata and liked her as much as he respected her. He took offense at a threat to her life. "Received at headquarters?"

"No. At her home. So whoever sent it has access to information about her and how to circumvent our protocols."

Slowly he nodded. "Any message?"

"Yeah." Hawkeye paused. "Threats to take out people I care about, one at a time."

"The fuck?" Instead of sympathizing, Jacob switched to ops mode. He didn't do it on purpose—it was as immediate as it was instinctive. No doubt Hawkeye had counted on Jacob's reaction. "Anything else?"

"There was no specific request. No signature." Hawkeye paused. "I've got profilers taking a look at it. But there's not much to go on. Tech is analyzing writing and sentence structure, tracking down places the card could have come from. FBI has the powder at its lab. Profilers are trying to ascertain the type of person most likely to behave this way."

All the right things.

"But we don't have the resources to take care of our clients and have eyes on everyone who's a potential target."

At this point, there was no way to know how serious the threat was. A card was one thing, a physical attack was another.

"I don't give a fuck who comes for me."

Over the years, their line of work—cleaning up situations to keep secrets safe, protecting people and precious objects, even acting as paramilitary support operators overseas—had created a long list of enemies.

"But I can't risk the people I care about." Hawkeye reached into a pocket inside his jacket and pulled out a picture. "I need you to take care of her."

"Oh fuck no, man." Jacob could be a sounding board, analyze data, but he didn't have the time to return to babysitting services.

Undeterred, Hawkeye continued. "Her name's Elissa. Elissa Conroy. Twenty-eight. My plan was to have Agent Fagen move in with her and accompany her to work."

Makes logical sense. "And?"

"She refused. Then I decided I'd prefer for her to be away

from Denver, out of her normal routine in case anyone has been watching." After a moment's hesitation, Hawkeye slid the snapshot onto the table, facedown.

Hawkeye knew every one of Jacob's weaknesses. If he glanced at Elissa's face, the job would become personal. She wouldn't be a random woman he could ignore.

Jacob looked across the expanse of the room, at the two men talking trash at the nearby pool table. Above them, a neon beer sign dangled from a tired-looking nail. The paint was peeling from the shabby wall, and the red glare from the light made the atmosphere all the more depressing.

"Her parents own a pub. Right now, she's running it on their behalf while they're back home in Ireland for a well-deserved vacation. Her father has just recovered from a bout with cancer, and they're celebrating his recovery."

Of course Hawkeye crafted a compelling narrative. He knew how to motivate people, be it through their heartstrings or sense of justice. At times, he'd stoke anger. His ability to get people to do what he wanted was his biggest strength as well as his greatest failing.

Never had his powers of persuasion been more on display than when he'd gotten his Army Ranger team out of Peru, despite the overwhelming odds.

From the beginning, the mission had been FUBAR—fucked up beyond all recognition. They sustained enough casualties to decimate even the strongest and bravest. Relentlessly Hawkeye had urged each soldier on. Despite his own injuries, Hawkeye had carried one man miles to the extraction point.

What happened immediately after that would haunt Hawkeye and Jacob to the end of their days, and it created a bond each would take to the grave.

"You've had some time on the ranch. I assume you're a hundred percent?"

Physically, yes. But part of him would always be in that South American jungle, trying to figure out what had gone so horribly fucking wrong.

Hawkeye nudged the photograph a little closer to Jacob.

"Who is she to you?"

Hawkeye hesitated long enough to capture Jacob's interest.

"Someone I used to know."

Jacob studied his friend intently. "Used to?"

Hawkeye shrugged. "It was a long time ago. Right after we got back from Peru." He stared at the photo. "She helped me through the rough patch."

Tension made Hawkeye's voice rough, and he cleared his throat.

"Shit." Jacob cursed himself for not walking out the moment Hawkeye asked for help. "It—whatever it was between you—is in the past?"

"Yeah. She's a smart woman, recognized damaged goods and was astute enough not to follow when I walked away." He shrugged. "To tell the truth, she's too damn good for me. We both knew it."

"It's over?"

"There never was anything significant. She's a friend. Nothing more. But if anyone's intent on hurting me..." With great deliberation, Hawkeye flipped over the picture.

Jacob couldn't help himself. He looked.

The woman was breathtaking. She was seated on a white-painted carousel horse, arms wrapped around its shiny brass pole. Dark, wavy hair teased her shoulders. But it was her eyes that stopped him cold.

He was a practical man more accustomed to making life-and-death decisions than indulging in fanciful poetry, but that particular shade of blue made him think of the columbines that carpeted the ranch's meadow each summer.

Her smile radiated a joy that he wasn't sure he'd ever experienced. Longing—hot and swift—ripped through him. Ruthlessly he shoved the unfamiliar emotion away. He was seated across from Hawkeye, discussing a job. Nothing more. If he accepted the assignment, it would be his responsibility to keep her safe and ensure she had plenty to smile about in the future.

"After this, Commander Walker, we'll call it even."

"Even from you, that's a fucking cheap shot." Jacob didn't need the reminder of how much he owed Hawkeye. Nothing would ever be *even* after the way the man rescued Jacob's mother from the inside of a Mexican jail cell.

Unable to stop himself, Jacob picked up the photo. Hawkeye's gamble—his drive deep into the Colorado mountains—had paid off. Jacob couldn't walk away. Elissa wasn't a random client. She was a woman who'd shown compassion to Hawkeye, and that shouldn't have put her at risk.

With a silent vow that he'd care for her until the shitstorm passed, Jacob tucked the picture inside his shirt pocket.

Hawkeye lifted his shot glass, then downed his whiskey in a single swallow.

"Sir? It's closing time." Elissa summoned a false, I'm-not-exhausted smile for the cowboy sitting alone at a table for two in her mom and dad's Denver-area pub. The man had been there for hours, his back to the wall. From time to time, he'd glance at the baseball game on the television, but for the most part, he watched other customers coming and going. More than once, she was aware of his focused gaze on her as she worked.

When he arrived, he asked for a soda water with lime.

Nothing stronger. Minutes before the kitchen closed, he ordered the pub's famous fish and chips.

Throughout the evening, he hadn't engaged with her attempts at conversation, and he paid his bill—in cash, with a generous tip—before last call.

Now he was the last remaining customer, and she wanted him to leave so she could lock up, head for home. She needed a long, hot bath, doused with a generous helping of her favorite lavender Epsom salts.

If she were lucky, she'd fall asleep quickly and manage a few hours of deep sleep before the alarm shrieked, dragging her out of bed. After all, she still had to run her own business while taking care of the bar.

Over the past few days, exhaustion had made her mentally plan a vacation, far away from Colorado. Maybe a remote tropical island where she could rest and bask in the sun. A swim-up bar would be nice, and so would a beachside massage beneath a palm tree.

But she was still stuck in reality. She had to complete the closing checklist, and that meant dispensing with the final, reluctant-to-leave guest.

With a forced half smile, she tried again. "Sir?"

The man tipped the brim of his cowboy hat, allowing her to get a good look at his face.

She pressed her hand to her mouth to stifle a gasp.

He was gorgeous. Not just classically handsome, but drop-dead, movie star gorgeous.

His square jaw was shadowed with stubble, but that enhanced the sharpness of his features. And his eyes... They were bright green, reminding her of a malachite gemstone she'd seen in a tourist shop.

In a leisurely perusal, he swept his gaze up her body, starting with her sensible shoes, then moving up her thighs, taking in the curve of her hips, then the swell of her suddenly aching breasts.

When their gazes met, she was helplessly ensnared, riveted by his intensity.

The silence stretched, and she cleared her throat. She was usually a total professional, accustomed to dealing with loners, as well as groups out celebrating and being rowdy, or even the occasional customer in search of a therapist while drowning their sorrows. But this raw, physical man left her twitterpated, her pulse racing while her imagination soared on hungry, sexual wings.

Andrew, the barback, switched off some of the lights, jolting her. After shaking her head, she asserted herself. "It's closing time, sir."

"Yes, ma'am." The cowboy stood, the legs of his chair scraping against the wooden floor. "I'll be going, then."

His voice was deep and rich, resonating through her. It invited trust even as it hinted at intimacy.

An involuntary spark of need raced up her spine.

Forcing herself to ignore it, she followed him to the exit. Instead of leaving, he paused.

They stood so close that she inhaled his scent, that of untamed open spaces. She tried to move away but was rooted to the spot. She was ensnared by his masculine force field—an intoxicating mixture of raw dominance and constrained power.

Desire lay like smoke in his eyes. In a response as old as time, pheromones stampeded through her. She ached to know him, to feel his strong arms wrap around her, to have his hips grinding against hers as he claimed her hard.

Dear God, what is wrong with me?

It had been too long since she'd been with a lover, but this cowboy was the type of man who'd turn her inside out if she let him. And she was too smart for that.

"Ma'am." Finally he thumbed the brim of his hat in a casual, respectful farewell that made her wonder if she'd imagined what had just happened between them.

"Thanks for coming in." Her response was automatic.

"I'll see you soon." Conviction as well as promise laced his words, and it shocked her how much she hoped he meant it.

After locking the door behind him, she stood in place for a few moments, watching him climb into his nondescript black pickup truck. It resembled a thousand others on the road, in stark contrast to its intense, unforgettable owner.

The barback tugged the chain to turn off the Open sign, reminding her of the chores still ahead of her.

It was past time to shove away thoughts of the stranger.

She checked her watch. A few minutes after one a.m.

It had been a long day. *Another* long day. With her parents still on vacation, the responsibility for running the pub had fallen to her. That wouldn't have been so bad, but Mary, the nighttime manager, had called in sick. And Elissa's freelance graphic project was due at the end of the week. Sleep had been in short supply for the past month.

Month?

Actually, it had been more than a year. Her father's cancer diagnosis had upended her family's world. The emotional turmoil had taken its toll as they all fought through the terrifying uncertainty and fear.

After his final chemotherapy treatment, her parents had departed for a much-needed break.

Andrew continued walking through the area, switching off the neon beer signs. "Everything's done. Clean and ready for tomorrow."

"Not sure how I would have managed without you." For the first time ever, he'd ended up waiting on several customers, and he'd done a good job. "Why don't you go ahead and leave?"

"I'll wait until you're done and walk you to your car."

"That's okay." She shook her head. It had been busier than usual for a Tuesday, more like she'd expect closer to the weekend. "I still have to reconcile the cash register, and that will take some time. You worked your ass off this evening. Go see your girlfriend."

"It's our one-month date-iversary. I didn't know that was a thing until this morning, and she warned me I better not screw it up." Clearly besotted, he grinned. "I don't mind staying, though, for a few more minutes."

"Go."

He glanced toward the rear exit. "If you're sure…"

"It's your date-iversary. *Go.*" She made a sweeping motion with her hand.

Grinning, she turned the deadbolt once he left.

After turning off the main dining room lights, Elissa retreated to the tiny management office. She sank into the old military-surplus style leather chair behind the metal desk. Determined to ignore the clock on the wall, she counted the cash, balanced the register, then ran the credit card settlement.

Once everything was done and the bank deposit was locked in the safe, she sighed, part in relief, part in satisfaction.

Finally.

As usual, she straightened the desktop and gave the office a final glance to be sure everything was where it needed to be.

Satisfied, she released her hair from its ponytail and fed her fingers through the strands to separate them, part of her ritual for ending the workday and easing into her off time.

Then she reached for her lightweight jacket. Even though it was summer, Colorado could still hold a chill after the sun set. Finally she slung her purse over her shoulder before plucking her keyring from a hook in the wall.

She let herself out the door, then secured the deadbolt behind her.

There were only a handful of vehicles in the parking lot, and she headed toward hers at a quick clip.

As she neared it, a figure detached itself from the adjoining building.

She struggled for calm, telling herself that the person wasn't heading toward her. But as she broke into a jog, so did the figure.

Frantically she ran, hitting the remote control to unlock the car, praying she could make it to safety before the assailant reached her. As she grasped the door handle, he crowded behind her, pressing her against the side of the vehicle.

"Get away from me!"

When he didn't, she screamed.

"Calm down."

Fuck. She recognized his gruff voice. *The cowboy.* For a moment, she went still. But when he pressed her harder against the car, fear flared, and she instinctively fought back. "Get the hell off me!"

He was unyielding, and her strength was no match for his.

"Hawkeye sent me."

Elissa froze. *Hawkeye?*

Of course he'd sent someone. She should have expected it when she refused to let him provide her with a bodyguard.

Years before, she'd met the wounded military man when he returned from an overseas mission. The first few times he'd come into the pub, he'd been quiet, drinking whiskey neat, staring at a wall while occasionally flinching.

They'd gone out a number of times, and she'd cared about

him. But no matter how hard she tried, she couldn't connect with him on an emotional level. He kept more secrets than he shared. But the one thing she learned was that the need for revenge consumed his every waking thought. In the end, it had been impossible to have any kind of relationship with him.

When he informed her that he'd started Hawkeye Security, she wasn't surprised. And when he came to say goodbye, she tearfully stroked his cheek while wishing him well.

She had been stunned when he called her to tell her she was at risk. Someone from his past threatened the people he cared about. Before hanging up, she dismissed his ridiculous concerns. Their halfhearted relationship was so far in the past that no one could possibly believe that she meant anything to Hawkeye.

"You're going to need to come with me."

"Oh hell no." Her earlier attraction to the stranger had vanished, replaced by anger. She made her own choices and didn't appreciate his heavy-handed tactics. "Tell Hawkeye I said both of you should fuck off. Or better yet, I will."

"I'm not sure you understand." His breath was warm and threatening next to her ear.

And now she understood why he'd spent so many hours at that table. He'd been studying her, planning the best way to bend her to his will.

But Elissa answered to no man.

"You're in danger."

"I can take care of myself. Now get off me, you..." *What?* "Oaf."

"As soon as you give me your word that you'll get in my truck without creating a fuss."

Realizing physical resistance was futile, she allowed her body to go limp and concentrated on tamping down her adrenaline long enough to outwit him. She needed to think and escape his unbearable presence. "How about I'll go home and stay there?"

"Not happening."

"Look..." There was no way she would yield to this oversize, determined goon, even if he was pure masculine perfection. "I'll agree to have one of his employees stay with me."

"He made that offer. You turned it down."

Damn you both. Why hadn't she just agreed to Hawkeye's suggestions?

"Let me be clear, Elissa..."

Despite herself, the way he said her name, gently curled around the sibilant sound, made her nerves tingle.

"He made it my job to protect you, and he signed off on my plan."

"Care to fill me in?"

"Yeah. We'll go to my ranch until he gives the all-clear."

Unnerved, she shivered. "Ranch?" That was worse than she could have imagined, and fresh panic set in. "I demand to talk to Hawkeye this instant."

"Demand all you want, little lady."

She refused to leave town, the pub, and be somewhere remote for an indeterminate amount of time with the cowboy shadowing her twenty-four seven. "No. No." She shook her head. "It's impossible. I'm needed here. And Hawkeye knows it." Struggling for breath, she pushed back against him. "We can work something out, I'm sure."

"You can take it up with him."

"Now we're getting somewhere. Let me get my phone out of my purse." *And figure out how to get in my car and drive like hell.*

"Not until we're on the road." He looped his massive hands around her much smaller wrists and drew them behind her.

"Ouch! Release me immediately!"

Though he didn't hurt her, his grip was uncompromising. "As soon as you agree to get in my truck without struggling."

"Look, Mr.—" *God. I don't know your name.* And like the asshole he was, he didn't fill in the missing information.

"We're done talking."

She stamped her foot on his instep, and he didn't even grunt, frustrating the hell out of her.

"Please get in my truck, Elissa."

Since he was immovable, she tried another approach, pleading with his better self. "I'm begging you. Don't do this. Let me go home." Elissa turned her head, trying to see him over her shoulder. Because of his hat and the darkness of the moonless and cloud-filled sky, his expression was unreadable. "You can follow me to my place." The lie easily rolled off her tongue. Anything to get away.

"Within the next five seconds, you'll be given two options, Ms. Conroy. One, you can come with me willingly."

"And the other?"

"You can come with me unwillingly."

"Option C. None of the above." With all her might, she shoved back, but he tightened his grip to the point of hurting her.

As if on cue, a big black truck—his, no doubt—pulled into view. Since he didn't react, it obviously meant Hawkeye had sent more than one person to deal with her. "This is absurd."

The vehicle, with no lights on, pulled to a stop nearby.

"I'll need your keys, Ms. Conroy."

She shook her head in defiance.

"Always going to do things the hard way?"

Since he was still holding her wrists, it was ridiculously easy for him to pry apart her fingers and take the fob from her.

"Has anyone ever told you that you're annoying as hell?"

A woman slid from the cab of the still-running pickup

and left the driver's side door open a crack. A gentle chime echoed around them, while light spilled from the interior, allowing Elissa to make out a few of the new arrival's features.

Dressed all in black, she was about the same height and build as Elissa. She even had long dark hair.

"Perimeter is still clear." Then in a cheery voice, she went on. "I see you haven't lost your way with the ladies, Commander."

He growled, all alpha male and frustration. "You're here to help, Fagan."

"That's exactly what I'm doing."

The cowboy eased his hold a little.

"Sorry for the caveman's actions, ma'am. I'm Agent Kayla Fagan. And I'm afraid Commander Walker needs a remedial training class in diplomacy."

Walker. First name? Or last? "Diplomacy? Is that what you call an abduction?"

He remained implacable. "I have my orders, and Ms. Conroy wasn't interested in talking."

Bastard. "His behavior needs to be reported to Hawkeye."

"I'll let you do that yourself," Kayla replied. "But honestly, I'd like to listen in."

"Get out of here, Fagan." He kept his body against hers while somehow managing to toss her keys to Kayla.

"Wait! You look so much like me you could be my double."

"That's the plan. Fagan will make it appear as if you're following your normal routine this evening while we get away. When we're on the road, you can talk to Hawkeye and make a strategic plan for opening the bar." Walker's tone was uncompromising.

The infuriating men had planned out everything.

Kayla opened the car door and slid into the driver's seat.

"Time's up, ma'am."

"Could you be any more condescending?"

"As I said, we can do this the hard way or the easy way. Your choice."

Determinedly Elissa set her chin. "I'm not going with you."

In a move so calculated and fast that she had no time to react, he took her purse from her, then yanked her around to face him. As if he'd done it a million times, he swept her off her feet, then hauled her into the air.

The Neanderthal tossed her over his shoulder, and she landed against his rigid body with so much force that breath rushed out of her lungs, stunning her into silence.

"The hard way it is."

CHAPTER TWO

HAWKEYE

"Go buy yourself a one-way ticket straight to hell." In the darkness of the truck's interior, Elissa glared at her captor. A minute ago, they'd pulled into a twenty-four-hour fuel stop, and he'd parked away from security cameras, in the shadows from the lights. Then he'd outlined his rules—rules she had no intention of following. "I mean it. There's no way —no fucking way—that you're going into the bathroom with me."

As implacable as usual, he regarded her. "In that case, we'll continue on. You can pee on the side of the road, but that won't be happening until we leave I-70." He lifted a shoulder in a small shrug, indicating he didn't give a damn whichever decision she made. "Hawkeye would prefer we limit law enforcement contact, and that's always a possibility if I pull over onto the side of the road. We should have our story straight. Could always say you're my pregnant wife who couldn't wait for the next town."

With a gasp, she folded her arms across her middle.

During the twenty minutes they'd been driving, he remained mostly silent, responding to her questions with irritating-as-hell half answers. He refused to let her have her purse or her phone. Other than saying that they were driving toward his ranch and that it was located in Colorado, he hadn't provided any further details.

"I don't want to lose time. Make a decision."

Commander Walker had already proven he was a hardass. Things were going to be his way or his way. Maddening.

While she didn't need the facilities right away, it was only a matter of time. And this place, on the far western side of the city, was the last reliably clean restroom for miles. "Fine."

With a tight nod, he reached into the back to grab a duffel bag. "There's some clothes in there for you."

"I'm not—"

"If you want to get out of this truck, you are."

She wasn't sure which one of them to kill first. Her kidnapper or Hawkeye. Either way, the act was going to be joyful.

"Time's ticking."

Elissa pulled out a sweatshirt and tugged it over her head. It was at least two sizes too large. The shoulder seams drooped down her arms, and the bottom would probably hit the tops of her thighs.

"Now the hat."

At least she liked the black cap with a bright purple baseball team logo on it.

Once she had it in place, he shook his head. "Can you do something with your hair?"

"Like what?"

"Stuff it under there or something."

Hurriedly she made a ponytail and threaded it through the opening in the back.

"Still too long. Recognizable."

Elissa sighed as she removed the hat. "I'm not sure what else to do." Thinking fast, she fashioned a makeshift bun and then took his advice and pulled on the hat. "No one does this. It looks ridiculous—lumpy."

"This isn't about fashion, ma'am." He cocked his head to one side to study her. "Pull the brim lower on your forehead."

"Look, Mr. Walker, I'm not cut out for this secret agent shit." Which had been one of the many reasons she and Hawkeye never had a real relationship.

"Save your breath. I'm about out of patience."

"You're almost out of patience? It isn't your life that's just been turned upside down."

"No?" The single word was quiet, but chilling. "Hawkeye gets what he wants."

Did that mean he was as reluctant as she was?

She shook her head. He was an agent—she was his mission. Nothing more.

He tucked a few loose strands of hair away, brushing her cheekbone.

Her reactions turned sluggish as his scent washed over her.

For a moment, neither spoke. Something primal—dangerous—pulsed between them.

Then, as if remembering himself, Jacob cleared his throat and glanced away from her. "There's a car pulling in on our left. Appears to have two occupants."

The abruptness edging his voice made her scoot away a little.

"We'll follow them in. Stay close. We want to make it appear we're a party of four. Got it?"

She sighed. "Is this all really necessary?"

"The boss says so. If you'd agreed to have a bodyguard when he suggested it, you could have avoided all of this."

Anger and frustration collided, making her vocal cords tight. "So it's my fault?"

Instead of responding, he kept his focus on the other

vehicle. "Be ready to move. When we're inside, head straight for the ladies' room. No stopping. Avoid the cash registers because of cameras. Don't touch anything. I've got plenty of food and water for us, enough to hold us till morning."

Are you planning to drive all night?

He kept his gaze on the car next to them. "On my mark, exit the vehicle."

Despite her insistence that this was nonsense, her heart was beating furiously, and she was even paranoid enough to check her mirrors for potential threats.

"Ready?"

Elissa nodded.

The other couple opened their doors.

"Let's roll."

Within moments, they entered the convenience store.

"Normal pace," he cautioned as they followed the signs toward the back wall. When they reached the bathroom, he held up a hand. "Wait here."

Using his foot, he pushed the door open.

As if that isn't suspicious.

After a few seconds, he returned. "Clear. Be as fast as you can."

In record time, she rejoined Commander Walker.

The woman who'd walked in before them handed a package of potato chips to her companion, then started toward the bathroom.

He nudged Elissa down a different aisle, then hurried her back outside.

In record time, he topped off the gas tank before accelerating down the on-ramp, sliding into traffic at the exact posted speed limit.

As they climbed into the mountains, leaving the metro area behind them, he looked in the rearview mirror, then loosened his grip on the steering wheel. Until that moment she hadn't realized how tense he was.

His phone rang, and Hawkeye's name appeared on the screen that had been showing a map.

Without saying anything, Commander Walker pushed the button to answer the call.

"Phase one of Operation Wildflower is underway, I presume?" Hawkeye's calm, almost cheerful voice filled the cabin.

"Operation Wildflower?" she repeated.

"I'll explain it to you later." Jacob slid her a glance before refocusing on the road and his conversation with Hawkeye. "Affirmative. Extraction complete. You already know that."

"Fagan had a couple of things to say about our client and your, ahem, lack of diplomacy."

"Stop with that word. I think you mean manhandling." Irritated, she scowled. How dare they talk about her as if she weren't there. "Actually the more appropriate term would be kidnapping."

"Hello, Elissa."

At one time, Hawkeye's voice had been as familiar as her own, until she realized he'd never allowed her to glimpse beyond a carefully constructed facade that hid his emotional pain and broken pieces.

"Commander Walker is one of the finest individuals I've ever known."

If she wasn't so annoyed, the words of praise might have meant something to her. "Is that supposed to make this all better?"

"Besides myself, he's the only one I trust with your life."

At the jagged note of emotion in his voice, her shoulders rolled forward. Whether she believed she was at risk or not, he did. "I hate this cloak-and-dagger stuff."

"And I hate that you're mixed up in it. I'll never forgive myself."

Even though she wanted to be mad, she couldn't be. But that didn't give him—or anyone else—permission to upend her entire world. "You know what's going on in my life, right? Let's be reasonable."

"Yesterday you refused."

"I've changed my mind." She blew out a wisp of breath. "Kayla is welcome to stay with me. I have an extra bedroom. And that way I can go back to work—"

"No." The two men spoke in unison, making her rub her temple to ward off the growing headache.

She should have already been in bed.

"Everything is covered at the pub."

Exhaustion evaporated. *"What?"*

"I talked to your parents and apprised them of the situation. They're being provided with hourly updates."

"How dare you?" Fury, white and blinding, flashed through her. She leaned forward, and the seatbelt grabbed her, preventing further movement. "What the hell is wrong with you? My dad can't handle that kind of stress."

"Patrick is stronger than you think. His only concern is your safety, and he immediately set about providing a solution to the problem. Your manager, Mary, says she's feeling better, and she intends to return to work tomorrow."

She exhaled her relief.

"Your dad was also able to get hold of Joseph. He's agreed to take the day shifts."

That news shaved the edges off Elissa's biggest concerns. Joseph had spent a number of years working for them and occasionally still picked up a few shifts. He knew Conroy Pub almost as well as she did, and he had earned her trust. Still, she hated that Hawkeye had upended so many people's lives.

As if he'd read her mind, Hawkeye spoke again, this time, more softly. "I know you're not happy. None of this would have been necessary if you'd have cooperated when I asked you to."

The same argument. Again. She sank back into the seat.

"There's a package waiting for you at the ranch. Some shoes and clothes, along with a secure cell phone—you'll be able to call your parents as soon as you arrive. You'll also be provided with a Bonds computer."

"Seriously?" Even though she wouldn't admit it, she was impressed. Because of her demanding graphic arts business, she'd lusted after one for years, but she'd never had that kind of money. Regardless, that wasn't the point. Right now, she needed her own equipment. "My software and files are on my desktop."

"You'll find everything already loaded on the new system. Bonds himself handled it."

She blinked. *"What?* Are you kidding me? You actually know Julien Bonds?" The genius of all things electronic. "And why would he do something like that?"

"We go back. And he loves getting involved in other people's lives. World-class meddler."

Even after all these years, Hawkeye still surprised her.

"Everything that was on your machine has been loaded on to your new computer."

"Wait." *God, no.* Her pulse stuttered, and when she managed to speak again, her words were a croaked whisper. *"All* of it?"

"All of it." Hawkeye cleared his throat. "Bonds said there was some kinky shit on there."

Unable to breathe, she stared straight ahead into the abyss of an endless highway.

"Kinky shit?"

She sensed that Jacob glanced at her, but she didn't look

in his direction. Instead, she wished the vehicle's undercarriage would open up so she could sink through it. No one had a right to look at her personal gallery, let alone comment on the contents.

"Elissa?" Jacob asked.

Desperately she searched for an explanation. "Those pictures... It was... Uhm... A project. For a client. Sworn to secrecy." The lie was the best she could come up with. No way was she confessing—to either one of these men—that the images were created from her own line drawings and inspired by her own vivid imagination.

"Bonds said he was impressed, that you have real talent." Surprise was etched in Hawkeye's tone. Despite the time they'd spent together, there was a lot he didn't know about her. "He suggested you consider showing it."

Not even if hell freezes over and starts selling the ice. She would never reveal her most intimate self to the world.

"You're welcome to get in contact with him. He has some recommendations."

"Thanks, but no." Even if she didn't have her own hesitations, she doubted there was a gallery on the planet interested in hanging her kind of paintings. "Let's get back to the previous conversation, please."

"I'll be in touch tomorrow."

Of course the asshole of all assholes had continued talking as if she hadn't said anything.

"I assure you that every resource is committed to this situation. Follow Commander Walker's orders, and we'll have you home before you know it."

The connection ended.

"I hate him."

In the darkness, her abductor looked at her.

"I hate this."

"In your place, so would I. It takes a special person to be

comfortable with this type of uncertainty."

Jacob's comments, uttered without even a ripple of emotion, intrigued her. "And you are?"

He was silent for so long that she wasn't sure he'd answer. "It comes from practice."

"Do you always speak so damn cryptically?" Like Hawkeye. Hadn't she learned a lesson about trying to communicate with military men?

"It's been safer that way."

"Well, after this is over, you'll never have to see me again, right? And it's not like I'd tell anyone anything that you said."

"The army teaches you a lot. At the time, I saw it as the only way out of a small town, the responsibilities of ranch life. I wanted adventure. You know, jumping out of helicopters, knocking down doors in a hail of gunfire."

She angled herself toward him. "You did all that?"

"Yeah." He shrugged "And more."

"Did you like it?"

"Not as much as I imagined I would. The adrenaline? That's fucking addictive. But I learned a lot that I never expected. Discipline. Patience—endless days, even weeks of waiting. Survival skills. Sleeping when I could, wherever I could. Eating even when I wasn't hungry, existing on soup for days when it was the only thing available." He adjusted one of the air-conditioning vents. "I learned how to make a plan and how to execute a new one when the first failed."

"Like throwing me over your shoulder?"

"I asked nicely."

"That's not how I remember it."

"Hmm."

They settled into silence, and she turned over the events that had unfurled since Hawkeye had called the day before. If only she had made different decisions when he said she needed protection. But at the time, she hadn't believed the threat was real. Even now, she wasn't sure it was.

Some time later, the cowboy exited the interstate. "Don't you think it's time you tell me where we're going? You have my phone, so it's not like I can contact anyone."

"The Starlight Mountain Ranch."

"It's yours?"

"Yeah." He paused for so long she wasn't sure he'd go on. "Fourth generation."

More intrigued than ever, she turned as much as she could to face him. Too bad there wasn't a little more ambient light so she could read his expressions. "And you live there with family?"

"It's just me. I'm the last one."

"I'm sorry to hear that." Her family meant everything to her. Her dad's recent health battle had only brought them closer together. She didn't like to imagine a future without them in it.

"I've had some time to get used to it."

"Is it a big place?"

"Depends on how you define that. Been added to throughout the years. The entire holding is around eight thousand acres."

"And are you ever going to tell me where it is?"

"Not far from Steamboat Springs. About twenty-five minutes south. On Trout Creek, a tributary of the Yampa River."

It was a beautiful area of the state, one she'd visited a few times. "We spent a couple of Christmases at one of the resorts near there."

"Good memories?"

They were…a reminder of a time when life was simpler, when they'd been together as a family, away from the responsibilities of running a business, and they'd played cards and board games, worked a few jigsaw puzzles, then spent evenings sipping hot chocolate in front of a crackling fire. "That's where I learned to ski and ice skate."

"You might enjoy yourself at the ranch."

"Vacations generally don't include having a jailer."

He glanced toward her. "Think of me as a protective friend."

The way she'd already responded to him made that idea laughable. "I don't even know who you are. I mean, beyond Commander Walker. Are you like Hawkeye, no first name, no last name?"

"It's Jacob."

"That's nice." Strong. It suited him. "Is it a family name?"

"No. It was one of my mother's few contributions to childrearing before she disappeared from my life. Haven't had any contact with her since..." He paused, as if deliberating how much to reveal. When he continued, his tone was flat. "It's been a long time."

"Oh God." The more she knew about him, the more he wound his way into her emotions. To keep herself safe, she couldn't let that happen. "That had to have hurt."

"My grandparents made sure I didn't miss her much."

Was that true, though? "Is she still alive?"

"Yeah." He set his jaw and turned on the radio, telling her the conversation was over.

Over the next hour and a half, she dozed, only to be jolted awake when he drove over a cattle guard.

"Sorry about that, Sleeping Beauty."

She blinked and forced herself to sit up a little straighter. "I wish I could see the surroundings."

"I'll give you a tour tomorrow. Or, rather, later today."

Jacob stopped in front of a massive iron gate. The truck's headlights allowed her to make out an ornate *W* in the middle.

He pressed a button on the dashboard, and the entrance swung open.

They continued along a dirt road for several minutes before the house came into view, fully lit. The home, constructed from beautiful pine logs, was massive, with several different wings. Numerous cozy-looking chimneys climbed toward the sky. "This is stunning."

"It's big. Too big for one person. My great-grandparents had a large family. And they took care of the ranch hands. It was a gathering place."

He pulled to a stop, and she gratefully climbed down from the passenger side. In the distance, the sun was casting its first rays, painting a few clouds pink.

Jacob grabbed his duffel bag before pressing a button on the remote to lock the vehicle. "After you."

She climbed the five steps to the porch. A swing, covered in pillows, hung near the door. Two Adirondack chairs were angled so they faced the distant mountain peak.

It appeared to be a perfect spot to sit and read.

Which she'd probably have plenty of time to do. Her stomach twisted into a sudden knot of resigned annoyance.

A loud hiss ripped through the still morning air. She glanced back at Jacob. "Uhm, do you have mountain lions or something out here?"

"Or something."

Suddenly, a massive animal leaped up the steps in a single movement, landing next to her. Screaming, she jumped sideways.

The creature crouched down, still hissing, staring at her. Contemplating if she was going to be breakfast? "Is that a lynx or something?"

"No. It's a Waffle."

"What is it, exactly?"

"A cat. Maine Coon, we think. She showed up one day as

a kitten and refused to leave. We had no idea she'd get so big or be so loud. The vet says that breed vocalize more than others. Lucky us."

"Interesting name."

"Well, my housekeeper's little girl dreamed it up because of the cat's various markings. She looks like a waffle with syrup on it. And whipped cream on the nose."

"I can see it." For the first time in hours, her tension eased, and she smiled.

He shrugged. "Better than Pancake, I suppose."

"You said you have a chef?"

"I like to eat, and I don't always have time to cook."

Waffle hissed again.

"She's harmless."

Elissa crouched, and the fur on the back of Waffle's neck stood on end—then she arched her back and moved back several feet. "Harmless? Are you sure about that?"

"You could say she has an interesting personality."

The moment Jacob stepped on the porch, the feline dashed toward him, then wound herself between his legs, rubbing and purring. "At least she's got good taste in humans."

Elissa rolled her eyes as she stood. "That's up for debate."

"She's not fond of Hawkeye."

"In that case, I like her more and more."

With a grin, Jacob reached across her to enter a code on the keypad and opened the door. "Seven, six, three, nine, five, two."

"What?"

"The security code."

"You mean I'm allowed to leave?"

"Of course. Despite what you said, I'm not your jailer, Elissa."

She frowned at him. "So I can go to Steamboat for a cappuccino? Maybe do a little shopping?"

"If I'm with you."

Remembering the ridiculous maneuvers he'd gone through to protect her identity at the fuel stop, skepticism raced through her. "And you'll take me?"

"Sure." He shrugged. "Later in the week, if things remain calm."

"That's a carrot, right?"

"Meaning?"

"You know, management techniques. Carrot and the stick. Positive versus negative reinforcement. If you promise me a reward, maybe I'll behave better."

"Yeah. That's it. You figured me out." He studied her in silence.

Annoyingly, her feminine instincts stirred again. She blamed her exhaustion as well as the night's extraordinary events.

After some sleep, she'd be herself again, back in control. There was no way her abductor could be this tempting.

"Go ahead inside."

She took a couple of steps only to have Waffle dart past her. The animal jumped onto a nearby table, looked back at Elissa, and hissed again.

"Mind your manners," Jacob told the cat before closing the door and dumping his bag on the floor. He stroked a finger between the cat's ears, and she turned her head into his hand. "Ms. Conroy will be with us for the foreseeable future."

The cat hissed, not seeming any happier with the news than Elissa was.

"I'll show you around."

At lightning speed, Waffle dashed away.

Elissa followed him to the inviting yet cozy living room

with furniture arranged in a U shape. A large couch faced the flagstone patio and wide-open meadow. Another was placed in front of the oversize fireplace and television. She imagined sitting here and relaxing, maybe with a glass of wine.

Beyond it was a sliding glass door leading to the patio.

"The kitchen is through here."

Maybe because he was a bachelor and the home had been standing for so long, she expected it to be dated. Instead, it was modern, with restaurant-quality appliances and gorgeous marble countertops. "I could spend days in here. It's a chef's delight."

"Glad you approve. You're exactly right. Eric designed it himself."

"That's your chef, I assume?"

"It is. He comes in a couple of times a week." Jacob filled a bowl with cat food and placed it on the floor. From nowhere, Waffle appeared and delicately picked out a single piece of kibble. "He hopes I'll start entertaining one of these days. Maybe open the house to guests."

"Like a bed-and-breakfast type of thing?"

"I'd be the perfect host. Easygoing. Attentive as well as accommodating."

For a moment she stared at him. "You're joking, right?"

He held his neutral expression for a moment before his lips twitched.

"Was that an attempt at humor?" When he stole her away from her life, she'd seen him as a rigid, one-dimensional secret agent man. And then he'd revealed a glimpse of his childhood. The confounded cat liked him, and now this.

"Did it work?"

Elissa gave herself a mental shake. He might be more complex and vulnerable than she expected, but she was still here against her will. No way should she let her guard down.

"Help yourself to whatever you want. The housekeeper

keeps the kitchen stocked with food and plenty to drink."

Something to help take off the edge so she could fall asleep would be welcome. "Dare I hope you have wine?"

"Lady's choice. Red or white?"

"Something crisp, a little sweet. Maybe a chardonnay?"

He pulled out a bottle from a small refrigerator tucked beneath the island. "Will this work?"

Elissa recognized the label and grinned with satisfaction. As far as being kidnapped was concerned, maybe this wasn't so awful. "Do I thank you or Eric?"

"My experience with wine is limited. I've been told reds go with beef, while whites go with seafood or chicken. I have no idea about pink."

"I think you mean rosé."

"See what I mean? And then someone else told me to forget the rules and that you should drink whatever the hell you want." He extracted the cork. "I know slightly more about whiskey, and I definitely have preferences when it comes to beer." He offered her the drink.

"Thank you." She took a long, leisurely sip. Now if she had a bathtub to soak in, life would be complete.

"I'll show you to your room."

She followed him up the stairs into a large bedroom dominated by an oversize bed. The comforter was thick and fluffy, and at least ten pillows encouraged her to bury in and create a nest.

"The closet is this way."

On a shelf were two large boxes.

"As Hawkeye promised." Jacob opened one and pulled out a cell phone and offered it to her. "It's secure, and you can contact your parents at any time."

Elissa put down her wineglass to accept the device. It was fully charged, and there was already a text from her dad, letting her know they'd been updated on the situation, had things under control, and were anxious to talk to her as soon as she was able to call.

The message reassured her.

She typed a quick response, informing them she'd arrived safely and would be in touch soon.

"Obviously we'd prefer you not tell anyone else your whereabouts." Without waiting for a response, he continued the tour. "Your bathroom is over here."

Her mouth fell open. It was massive, luxurious, spa-like with a sophisticated-looking steam shower, and her greatest wish had been answered—a soaker tub. A long white robe hung from a hook on the back of the door. This was as classy as the best hotels she'd stayed at. "Are you kidding me?"

A sudden grin transformed his features, making him seem younger, somewhat less formidable. Standing this close, in intimate quarters, arousal galloped through her. "I take it you're not unhappy?"

This time, she was sure it wasn't just the lack of sleep that was affecting her hormones. It was also a result of the alcohol's slow burn.

Turning away from him, she cleared her throat. Unfortunately it didn't help to tame her heart's frantic response to his overwhelming masculinity.

She struggled to pretend this was a normal situation. "This is about the size of my entire apartment." And she wasn't sure she'd be able to return home after being cocooned in this kind of luxury. "Are you sure you haven't given me the master suite?"

"I'm downstairs. In another wing. I'll include it in tomorrow's tour of the grounds."

That sounded as dangerous as it was tempting.

"I'm sure you'll be safe here, but that button next to the light switch"—he pointed—"is for emergency situations. There's another on the nightstand. You'll find them in every room of the house. I'll be alerted twenty-four seven, no matter where I am. Don't hesitate to use it. I'd rather it be a false alarm than take a risk with your safety."

Hating the reminder of why she was here, she nodded.

"Sleep as late as you want. We're not on a time schedule."

"At this point, I might not see you until this evening."

"In that case we'll have dinner instead of breakfast. Good night."

He left, closing the door behind him.

She remained where she was, listening for his receding footsteps. They never came.

A full minute later, she toed off her shoes. She contemplated falling face-first onto the bed. But there was no way she could sleep in the clothes she'd worked in, traveled in.

A yawn overtook her, and she decided to take a shower rather than a bath since it would be faster.

Thoughtfully, a dispenser had been filled with shampoo, conditioner, and even lavender-scented soap.

After turning off the water, she wrapped her hair in a towel, then dried herself. Then, unable to resist, she snuggled into the warm, thick robe before crossing to the closet to see what Hawkeye had sent.

One box was filled with electronics, and the other contained her personal items. Cosmetics, hairbrushes, shoes, socks, jeans, shorts, tops for every possible temperature, jackets, sports bras, *panties...*

Dear God. Let it have been Kayla who'd gone through her dresser drawers.

Elissa dug to the bottom and found no pajamas.

No doubt it had been Hawkeye who selected everything. Damn it.

From somewhere close, the unmistakable rumble of Jacob's voice reached her. Curious, and hoping she could borrow a T-shirt, she left the room.

Down the hallway, a light blazed, and she walked toward it. *Like a moth to a flame?*

When she found Jacob, she froze.

He was seated behind a console, and in front of him were numerous large screens split into sections that contained a video feed. Most of the images were of the outdoors—the gate, dirt road, driveway, front door, sides of the house, and the patio. Others showed pictures of the home's interior, including the kitchen, living room, entryway, and a bedroom with a king-size bed with navy blue comforter. His?

"Elissa." He spoke without looking toward her.

How did he know she was there?

He tapped an icon and removed his headset. "Is there something you need?"

"Have you been spying on me?" She dragged the robe's lapels close together, as if that would protect her. "Are you some sort of sick pervert who gets his jollies out of something like that?"

"No." He spun in his chair, but he didn't get up. "To both of your questions."

"Oh." She exhaled her flare of indignation.

"Come here."

She didn't want to. Shouldn't. "I—"

"Come here."

Because of *that* tone, uncompromising in the same way as it had been when he'd tossed her over his shoulder and kidnapped her, she moved toward him, stopping when she was in front of him.

Even though he was seated, he radiated an aura of command, and goose bumps chilled her arms.

"Your opinion of me is clear. And somewhat unfair. You have a certain degree of privacy while you're my guest."

At that, she scoffed. *"Guest?"*

"Use whatever term you prefer, Elissa. But I guarantee

you this—if you were my prisoner, things would be different."

She took a step back, but he prevented another by snagging one of her wrists with his massive hand.

"There's a room near mine. A whole lot less pleasant than the one I gave you. I spend a lot of time on the range, and I know a thing or two about ropes. It'd only take a few seconds to tie you up, maybe secure you to a bed."

Jesus. She shivered. What the hell was happening here? His words sparked fantasies, turning her insides molten.

"Or maybe you'd like that?"

Desperately she snatched her wrist away from him.

"This"—he turned toward his command post and pointed to a blank section on one of the screens—"is the feed from your room."

"Oh." What else did she say to that and her wild accusation?

"I don't spy on women, Elissa." He cocked his head to the side to look up at her.

He was close enough for her to be frighteningly fascinated by the pulse ticking at his temple. She'd either pissed him off or insulted him. Perhaps both. Maybe she should apologize, but in these extraordinary circumstances, she couldn't find the words.

"Believe it or not, I only associate with women who are willing."

And no doubt there were plenty of them. Not only was the man an alpha—he was gorgeous, protective, and apparently rich. "I shouldn't have jumped to conclusions."

"Thank you for that." The furrow between his eyebrows eased. "Apology accepted."

That was it? For two years, she'd been involved in a relationship with a man who was quick to anger, for the smallest of reasons. She'd had to earn his forgiveness. One time, he'd given her the silent treatment for days before ungenerously doling out his attention again.

Her parents and friends encouraged her to leave him. Once she did, it had taken her a long time to realize he'd used his temper to control her.

That Jacob offered forgiveness quickly and unconditionally left her reeling.

"You sought me out for a reason, presumably?"

"I..." She exhaled. The reason no longer seemed important. Needing space, she took a step away from him. "Hawkeye forgot to pack my pajamas."

"Hawkeye had nothing to do with it. The oversight was mine."

"Yours?" He'd gone through her lingerie drawer? The realization left her breathless. Had his selection been random? Or had he deliberately chosen things that appealed to him?

"Sleepwear never occurred to me."

Of course it hadn't. "Why? I mean..."

"Hawkeye sent a small team to your apartment. I gathered belongings. A technician backed up your computer after verifying there were no viruses on it."

"I guess I don't need to mention that it was password protected."

"A combination of your birthday and initials. Took about ten seconds to get in."

She sighed.

Jacob swiveled to switch to another set of videos. "This is your front door." He pointed to another screen. "And your street."

It was strangely fascinating to see a neighbor walking toward his car carrying a coffee mug.

"There's an app on your phone so that you can look anytime you want."

"Are there any cameras inside my place?"

He shook his head.

Thank God for that. "Do you or Hawkeye have any other nasty surprises in store for me?"

Once again, he turned toward her. "All of these precautions are because you matter to Hawkeye. Other clients pay premium prices for this kind of service."

"I'm supposed to be *grateful?*" Her life had become a surreal nightmare.

Rather than answer, he changed the subject. "Is there a reason you came looking for me? Did you need something? Companionship, perhaps?"

"Absolutely not." Never from him. "I was wondering if you, maybe, you know... The sleepwear you forgot to pack. Do you have a T-shirt I can borrow?"

"Yeah. Of course. In my room." He rolled his chair to the side, then turned and stood. "I'll get you one. Or you can help yourself."

Go in his room? She shook her head.

"I was heading downstairs anyway. Come with me."

It made sense. The suggestion was innocent enough. But every instinct screamed against that. He might actually have strong morals, but she'd glimpsed the wolf beneath that polished exterior.

"You're safe." He strode past her.

Her senses ignited, and in that instant she recognized the truth. She wasn't scared of him. She hungered for him. The power of her need terrified her.

When he started down the stairs, she followed, rationalizing that she was an adult. If he could behave, she could put a cage around her own attraction.

"This way."

His private wing of the house had a different aura. The woods were darker, and so were the colors. There were no pictures on the walls, and that was when she realized the ones in the entryway and living room were of landscapes, revealing nothing personal.

They passed a couple of closed doors. Was one of them protecting the room he'd threatened her with? The one she wouldn't want to stay in? "Were you kidding earlier? About ropes and such?"

"As you've noticed, I don't joke often."

She shivered.

Without hesitating, he continued through the open door of the master bedroom. After a misstep, she went in after him.

A gigantic four-poster bed barely took up any space. French doors opened to the patio, now bathed in soft morning light. Again, there were no pictures or clutter. It was stark. Sterile. As if he had no past, no present, and wanted to leave no mark on the world.

Or maybe she was being fanciful.

"All of my clothes are in the closet." He tossed his keys on top of a nightstand. "Help yourself."

That seemed really personal, but so was wearing his clothes. "You don't mind?"

"Not in the least."

Because he organized with military precision, it took no time to find exactly what she was looking for on a shelf.

Clutching a black T-shirt in front of her, she rejoined him.

He was pulling off his belt, and he stopped when he saw her.

"I, uhm… This will work." Heaven help her. Standing this close to Jacob in his room made arousal ripple through her, freezing her in place. Coming in here with him had been a horrible mistake. To save herself, she had to escape from his room. *Now.*

"You're welcome."

The sensual, intimate rumble in his voice short-circuited her brain cells, leaving her rooted to the spot.

As if compelled by the same madness that gripped her, he took a step toward her. "Elissa." He cupped her shoulders, his touch as gentle as it was reassuring.

She leaned into him, anticipating, hoping...

"Jesus." He took a breath and closed his eyes. When he opened them again, their gazes collided. She saw hunger in the dark green depths, combined with hesitancy and remnants of the pain she'd glimpsed earlier.

"We shouldn't."

He was right, but she thirsted too much to refuse him.

"You're my client." Possessively rather than painfully, he dug his fingers into her skin. "Mine to protect."

His words fanned a feminine response she'd never before experienced. Her heart raced, and the floor seemed to sway beneath her. Jacob Walker was as dangerous as he was irresistible. And she had to know what he tasted like. "Kiss me?" It was an invitation as much as a plea.

"Elissa..." But even as he shook his head, he continued to hold her as if he'd never let go. "These are unusual circumstances, and your emotions are likely heightened."

If the darkness of his eyes was any indication, he was not immune to her either.

"You might regret this."

"I know what I'm doing." The only thing she would regret was passing up this moment. "Kiss me."

Fire flared in his eyes. Then, with a groan, he brushed his lips across hers.

The fleeting touch wasn't enough. "Jacob..."

He drew her up onto her tiptoes and captured her mouth, seeking entrance.

This time there was nothing gentle about him. His tongue

sought and found hers. Tasting of temptation, he staked a claim, feeding one hand into the strands of her hair to ease back her head.

In response to his silent demand, she opened wider, granting him the access he demanded.

As their tongues danced, her knees weakened. Desperate for the support, she reached up to entwine her hands behind his neck.

His arousal pressed against her soft belly. She was open, exposed, vulnerable in a way she never had been before, and for that moment, she was his for the taking.

The kiss went on forever yet ended too soon.

Before releasing her, he gently bit her lower lip, leaving behind a tiny sting that would remind her of this moment.

"You're beautiful, Elissa. Everything I imagined." He touched her swollen lips. "And now I need you to go to your room and lock the door. Or else I will tie you to my bed for the rest of the night."

She gasped.

"Jesus. You have to leave." He walked to the door and stood beside it purposefully.

For a shocking, horrifying moment, she considered disobeying him.

"Please." His hoarse plea sounded as if it had been dragged through gravel, promising her he'd follow through with his threat if she didn't leave.

Sleeping with her kidnapper would be insanity. She told herself it was the situation, or maybe the wine, maybe the lateness of the hour, but she'd momentarily lost her head.

Still, on her way past him, she paused.

"No matter what, don't unlock your door for me."

She shivered, as much from the threat as from the power of her own sexual response to him.

CHAPTER THREE

HAWKEYE

Elissa needed tea. Or really, anything infused with caffeine, hot or cold, was fine.

She dropped her forearm over her eyes.

Even though the bed was comfortable, she hadn't managed to sleep for more than a few hours. The bright Colorado sun blasted the room, despite the fact that the blinds were closed. And the deadline to get designs over to her client was only a couple of days away, creating anxiety. Not that she needed more of that.

In flashes, memories of the previous night rushed through her mind, from the strange attraction at the pub, to the hardness of his body as he'd swept her from the ground and tossed her over his shoulder. Then…the kiss. Her lower lip still tingled from Jacob's passion.

What was worse was how close she'd come to asking him to tie her up.

As long as she could remember, she'd wanted to experiment with BDSM, but she'd never had a partner willing to explore with her. Jacob, on the other hand, had read her accurately, and she had no doubt he was capable of giving her everything she desired.

Yet he was the one man she dared not play with. It would lead to nothing other than heartache.

The craziness of the situation would be over soon, maybe in a few days. She'd go back to her life. No way could she become attached either physically or emotionally to another former military man who operated in the shadows.

But still, no matter how hard she tried to shove aside thoughts of last night or the stupidity of finishing what had started in his bedroom, the stronger and more tantalizing they became.

Frustrated, she flipped onto her stomach.

Despite her efforts to control her runaway fantasies, she imagined he actually had kept her in his room and tied her to his massive bed.

First, he would strip off her clothes and trail his fingers across her needy body. Once she was aroused, he'd pick her up and place her on the mattress. Then he'd exert his masculine dominance, securing her with ropes while she writhed, captured, unable to escape his sexual determination.

She'd gasp when he played with her pussy, and she'd silently beg him to take her. And when he did, it would be as powerful as a storm.

The pictures flashing like strobe lights through her brain made her clit throb.

She needed to orgasm.

Maybe that would put a stop to the stampede of impossible, tempting thoughts. Surrendering, just for the moment, she reached a hand beneath her pelvis and pressed against her clit.

She moaned into the pillow.

Then all of a sudden she was lost…in a fever of arousal, grinding her hips, seeking release. Elissa slipped two fingers inside herself, wishing instead that it was Jacob's massive cock filling her.

Faster and faster, she moved, thinking about the sight of him holding his belt, the leather tantalizing.

Within moments, she climaxed, screaming his name, praying he didn't hear her.

For moments afterward, she lay there, her breaths disjointed as she labored to return to reality.

The climax had been as swift as it was powerful. But shockingly, she was still thinking about Jacob.

What's wrong with me?

Elissa didn't masturbate often, and when she did, she was generally satisfied for days, maybe even a week. This internal hunger for a specific man was new. And she didn't like it. She wasn't the type of woman to think about sex all the time. Or, rather, she hadn't been until the cowboy uprooted her life.

Determinedly she punched her pillow into a different shape while telling herself to focus on something else. Like work. That was always her favorite refuge. She had to decide on the colors and fonts to communicate her client's brand. He was a motivational speaker, and she wanted something engaging, a bit bold to reflect his personality, but it also needed to invite trust. Meeting planners had to be confident when booking him.

In the distance, a door closed.

Did that mean Jacob had left the house?

If so, maybe it was safe to get her tea so she could hurry back to the sanctuary of her room.

Seizing the opportunity, she turned over, then climbed out of bed.

After pulling on a pair of leggings but not changing out of his T-shirt, she headed downstairs only to freeze once she reached the kitchen.

Jacob was there, leaning against the countertop, a mug in

hand. He wore a skimpy pair of swim trunks and nothing else. His short hair was wet and slicked back, while droplets of water clung to his broad chest.

As she watched, fascinated, unable to look away, one arrowed downward, stopping right above his waistband.

The man was a living Adonis.

Every muscle was chiseled, and he didn't carry an ounce of fat anywhere. Numerous scars attested to his rough life, feeding her curiosity. As crazy as it was, she hungered to know everything about him.

"Morning."

She looked up and met his gaze, flushing when she realized she'd been caught staring at him.

As if they shared a secret, he smiled, making him even more lethal to her senses.

She would have dressed properly before coming down if she'd realized he was in the house. Self-conscious, hyper-aware of his masculinity, she cleared her throat before pulling back her shoulders and pretending that this was a common experience.

"Did I wake you up?"

"No. I mean, not really. I heard a door close. I thought you'd left."

"Spent a few minutes in the hot tub, then had a swim."

She tucked wayward strands of hair behind her ears. Being in intimate quarters with a captor, especially after a sizzling kiss, was a new experience, and she had no idea how to act. She thought fast, struggling for some sort of normalcy. "I need to get some work done." If that was even possible.

"Can I get you a cup of coffee first? It's fresh."

"Tempting. But I was thinking about tea this morning." Besides, the stainless-steel carafe was on the counter next to him, and she didn't want to get that close.

"There should be some in the pantry."

The shelves were well stocked, including numerous boxes of tea, and she went straight for the Earl Grey. "Yesterday, you mentioned I have a new computer here?"

"Ready to set up anywhere you wish. You could share my office."

"Uh…" She frantically thought. "The kitchen table would be fine."

"There's an apartment above the garage. Originally it was a stable and bunkhouse, but I had it converted. It has great light. There's even a small kitchen and a desk. You might enjoy the space and feel like you have a little freedom."

A small mercy. "You mean I don't have to stay in the house with you all day?" Because she wasn't sure she could survive that.

"Of course not. I want you to be comfortable."

"As if."

He inclined his head in acknowledgment. "As much as possible, then." He took a drink. "You'll find an internet connection throughout the property, so you can work almost anywhere. The hot tub and pool are at your disposal as well."

"I didn't see a swimsuit in the box."

"You don't need one."

She notched up her chin. "I don't skinny-dip."

"Pity."

The atmosphere crackled around her, supercharged, like the moment right before lightning struck.

It was then that she noticed his trunks were dry. That meant either he'd changed—which was unlikely—or he'd put them on after he exited the pool. Had he been prowling around outside naked?

Heaven help me. There was no way she would ever get that image out of her mind.

"You can always wear a bra and panties, if your modesty matters."

Not that he'd packed any underwear that covered much. He'd skipped briefs in favor of thongs and boy shorts.

"The housekeeper isn't here today, and none of the ranch hands will head this direction without my prior approval. Hawkeye has a few agents stationed nearby, but your privacy will always be respected." He refilled his mug. "For the moment, it's just the two of us."

Just the two of us. His words unnerved her. Was there anything more dangerous to her senses? "Thank you for the offer, but I'll keep my clothes on."

His quick grin disarmed her.

How many dimensions were there to this man?

"Can I get you some breakfast?"

"Uhm…"

"I want to make sure I meet all your basic needs."

She blinked. Were they talking about food?

"Thought I'd treat you to my specialty. French toast stuffed with cream cheese and covered with strawberry topping."

On cue, her stomach grumbled. "If you're serious, yes. Please." In the mornings, Elissa generally grabbed a bagel. It required no effort, and she could eat at her desk while reading her emails and catching up on the news. "Is there anything I can do to help?"

"Just worry about your tea. Not one of my specialties."

Since she was helping out at the pub and had recently been spending her time serving others, having someone take care of her needs was the ultimate luxury.

While he whipped up some eggs and added sugar and vanilla along with a generous shake of cinnamon, she placed a cup of water in the microwave to heat up. She was careful not to bump into him, something that wasn't easy. His movements were efficient, but he was so large that he dwarfed the space.

Once her beverage was ready, she carried the cup to the far side of the island and slid onto one of the stools. This far apart, with an expanse of marble separating them, she shouldn't be aware of his every motion. Yet she knew exactly what he was doing, even without looking, as if her senses were supercharged.

He turned on two burners and straddled them with a griddle.

"Are you sure there's nothing I can do? Set the table, maybe?"

"That would be great. I thought we might eat on the patio. It's nice enough."

He told her where to find everything, and she once again took care to skirt by him without touching. With everything gathered on a tray, she fled from the house and her dangerous desire for him.

Outside, she released a breath, not just because she was away from him, but also because of the endless vista and the warmth of the sun on her bare skin.

The sky was a stunning shade of bright blue, and only a few wispy clouds floated by. The flagstones beneath her bare feet were warmer than she expected for so early in the summer. Numerous lounge chairs were scattered in various groupings and accented by huge potted plants and trees. Off to one side was a stone firepit with wicker furniture in front of it.

After arranging plates and silverware on the metal table, she made another trip for their beverages, and a final one for the strawberry topping. Then, since he was still cooking, she walked toward the gazebo at the edge of the patio. The lightest hint of a breeze stirred the late-morning air.

Her initial impression of the ranch hadn't prepared her for the actual experience of breathing in fresh Rocky Mountain air. In the distance, a single mountain dominated the landscape. Because she lived in suburban Denver, she rarely glimpsed an unobstructed view of anything. The landscape beckoned, making her want to explore her surroundings.

Just as quickly as the idea occurred to her, she shoved it away. Being here was temporary, and she'd never have the opportunity to return.

Inside the house, dishes clattered, signaling that Jacob was wrapping up, and she wandered to the pool area. The water rippled and reflected sunlight, making her wish he actually had packed a swimsuit for her.

When she reached the hot tub, she was unable to resist temptation, and she crouched to dip her hand into the warmth.

"You sure you don't want to get in?" he shouted from the back door.

And have him watch me walk around naked? "No." *Maybe.*

Her heart fluttering again, she met him at the table and sat down across from him. In addition to the French toast, he'd brought out a bottle of pure maple syrup and a platter of bacon. He was a man after her heart.

The meal was prepared perfectly. The bread had exactly the right amount of batter, and it was golden brown. A hint of the filling peeked out around the edges. "Looks amazing." She filled her plate, then took a bite and sighed. "Do you treat all your captives this well?"

"I prefer the term client. Or protectee." He snapped his fingers. "Wait. As I said before, guest is even better. It makes a difference to your experience. Therefore, service matters, which you know all about since your family is in the hospitality industry. We're hoping you'll leave Hawkeye a good review online and recommend us to your friends and family."

At his absurdity, she couldn't help but grin.

"I'm hoping you'll give us five stars for the Morning Star

Suite here at the Starlight Mountain Ranch. I trust the bed is comfortable enough?"

Seduced by the meal, his smile, the surroundings, and his banter, she played along. "Definitely. Exceeded my expectations." Which was true. "The fluffy robe is a nice touch. If I take it home, can you add the cost to my bill?"

"It's complimentary with every five-day stay."

How different would the experience be if she really were his guest here? Everything about the place was spectacular. Over the years, she'd paid a lot of money to relax and recharge at nearby lodges and spas, but she'd never had any of them to herself.

As they ate, he informed her the distant peak was named Saddle Mountain. Then he gave her the history of the ranch, including the struggles each generation had gone through to hold on to it.

"Ranching isn't easy. And the world isn't either. My great-grandparents lost their only son in a war. There are challenges with fluctuating beef prices, drought, fights over water rights. Weather. Always the weather. One thing my grandfather was interested in was cross-breeding. Our cattle can survive the harshest winters and terrain. Because of that, we sell them all over the country, including Montana and Wyoming."

"I didn't even know that was a thing."

"It took us years to get it where it is now. Still a long way to go. But his foresight has been the thing that has helped us hold on to the property."

She sipped from her now cool tea. "You love it here."

Before answering, he looked into the distance. "I didn't always." He pushed his empty plate aside. "It took being gone to appreciate my roots."

"Did you leave to work with Hawkeye?"

A red-tailed hawk screeched in the sky, then soared on a thermal.

"No. Much earlier than that. I joined the military right after college."

"So that's where the two of you met?"

"Yeah." He faced her again. "In another lifetime."

"Sometimes I think he never came back."

Jacob inclined his head to one side, watching her carefully. "You've known him a long time."

"No. I mean... As the calendar goes, yes. Years. But I don't know him at all." She shook her head. "For a little while, I thought maybe I did. Then one day he was gone. And I mean that literally. I saw him almost every day, and then...nothing."

Jacob fixed her with his intense gaze. "You were hurt?"

"Of course." A little lost. Bereft, but more than anything, confused. She'd become accustomed to Hawkeye coming into the pub late every afternoon. He'd spend hours there, staying until well after dark. They enjoyed deep conversation, and he'd taken her out for dinner on a couple of occasions. One moonless evening, after he'd walked her home, they shared a meaningful kiss on her front porch. She'd gone to bed wondering if their relationship would develop into something more substantial.

She never expected he'd leave without saying goodbye. Less than a week later, he called to say he was no longer in the state and had no plans to return. "I thought we were friends, but the truth was, he'd never let me in. He never mentioned his family or his life before the military. I know something happened in..." She paused, wondering if he'd fill in the details. "Peru or Ecuador, if I recall."

"Close enough."

So Jacob knew. Or he'd been there as well. "It was as if

he'd been at the pub physically, but somewhere else mentally."

"Yeah."

Jacob was slightly different. Just as strong. Rugged. Dangerous. But last night there'd been heat in his eyes. There'd been emotion in his voice when he commanded her to leave. It made him more complex, a little more human.

"He's worried about you." He steepled his index fingers. "Clearly you mean something to him."

She hesitated before replying. "Are you fishing for information, Jacob?"

"And if I am? Wondering what you mean to each other?"

Elissa sucked in a shallow breath. Asking about her entanglements indicated either a natural curiosity or something more. Since they'd kissed, she was willing to bet he wanted to be sure her relationship with his friend wouldn't come between them. Finally she exhaled. "To be honest, nothing other than friendship. When we met, I wondered if there might be something more." She shook her head. "There wasn't."

Because he allowed the silence to engulf them, she was compelled to continue. "That's why I'm frustrated by this whole thing. You know, the way you abducted me and—"

He winced, and she stopped talking.

"You've mentioned that once or twice."

"All I'm trying to say is that Hawkeye shouldn't be concerned for my well-being at all. No one really knew about us—not that there ever was an us." She shrugged. "You have to admit I have a point, though. Right? He's overreacting." She expected to garner sympathy or at least understanding. Instead, Jacob's features hardened, and shards of jade shot through his eyes.

"Hawkeye doesn't take chances with people who matter to him."

"God, Jacob. Have you listened to a single word I've said? *I don't matter to him*, and I never did."

"Someone may believe differently. And that's the only thing that matters."

With a clatter, she put her cup down. The conversation was going nowhere. Jacob was loyal to his friend rather than to her.

"I have my orders."

Like a good military man, he would follow them. Why had she hoped for anything different?

After a long pause, he finally spoke. "How much do you know about what's going on?"

"Nothing. Absolutely nothing." She exhaled her frustration. "I'm struggling with all this drama. In my place, would you take it seriously?"

"He has a right-hand woman." His tone was measured, as if deciding how much information to divulge.

"Are you talking about Ms. Inamorata?"

"So you do know her?"

Elissa desperately wanted to yank back her words. "You miss nothing."

"My life, and those of others, has depended on it."

"I swear to you, it's been a long time since I've seen Hawkeye." It was important to her that Jacob understood completely.

"And?"

Things were suddenly more complicated. They were having two different discussions. One about her relationship with his friend. Another where she was trying to convince Jacob to let her go back to her regular life. "About a year ago, Hawkeye was passing through Denver, and he stopped in the pub and ordered a whiskey, neat. I brought him the wrong brand. In the years since I'd seen him, he'd switched to something smoother and much more expensive. That's when we caught up."

Without responding, Jacob nodded.

Had her explanation satisfied him?

He tapped his fingers, as if contemplating how much to reveal. "Inamorata received a birthday card at her home, and there was white powder in it. Results have confirmed it was anthrax."

A chill rocked through Elissa, and she wrapped her arms around herself to ward it off. "Is she... Someone tried to..." *Oh no.* Despite herself, the news unnerved her. "Is she okay?"

"Yes. She was immediately started on antibiotics as a precaution, and there are no ill effects. In fact, she was furious at herself for opening the envelope and refused to take any time off work." He leveled a stare at her, and his eyes were icy enough to freeze her in place. "Whoever it is has already reached the upper levels of the company. We have no idea what kind of information he—or she—has access to." He paused. "It could be someone who works for the company."

For the first time, a tendril of doubt unfurled inside her. With determination, she tamped it down. No doubt the arrogant males surrounding her were overreacting. *But were they?*

"All of Hawkeye's resources are focused on this." His tone was as cold as it was detached.

"Jacob—"

"The sooner you accept reality and make yourself comfortable here, the easier this will be." He leaned toward her and imprisoned her gaze. "You're staying in protective custody until Hawkeye says otherwise. My decision is non-negotiable."

Even though Jacob made polite conversation through the rest of breakfast, his harsh words continued to echo in her ears. How was she supposed to be comfortable out here in the middle of nowhere, alone with a stranger who'd kissed her and haunted her dreams?

"Elissa?"

Since he was looking at her quizzically, she shook her head to clear it.

"I asked if you were finished eating."

"Yes. Thanks." She nodded, then, when he pushed back his chair and stood, followed suit.

Together, they cleared the table, then straightened the kitchen.

"I'll be in my office if you need anything." He inclined his head before walking away.

Under normal circumstances, she might have enjoyed his polite, old-fashioned charms. But she already knew what lay beneath the polished exterior.

Once the sound of his footsteps had vanished and silence shrouded her, she walked to the window and stared into the distance. Just yesterday, there hadn't been enough time to get everything done that she needed to. And now, the upcoming hours seemed to loom like an unpleasant specter.

Even more restless and uncertain than she had been before breakfast, she headed upstairs, quietly passing his office on the way to her bedroom.

She closed the door and then dialed her dad's phone number.

As the call connected, she paced the confines of her temporary bedroom. When she'd first arrived, the space seemed large and luxurious. Now it was claustrophobic, the walls closing in on her.

"Elissa, love!"

At the welcome sound of his voice, an emotional lifeline like it had always been, she collapsed her shoulders against the wall.

"I know you've been texting, and Hawkeye's been keeping us posted, but it's good to hear from you."

She fought for normalcy in order to reassure him. "How are things in Ireland?"

"We're at the airport."

"What? The airport?"

"Hawkeye chartered a plane for us. Can you imagine? We're waiting for our flight now."

The news shouldn't have surprised her, but it did. "There's no need to cut your trip short." They needed the break. Deserved it. "This will all be over soon." It had to be.

"It's all arranged. Hawkeye's having us picked up when we arrive at the Denver airport and assigning us a security agent."

A chill shot up her spine. *"What?"*

"It's out of an abundance of caution."

She exhaled a worried sigh. This was all too much. And if Hawkeye were truly that concerned, wouldn't her parents be safer if they were out of the country? "Dad. Seriously. Stay there."

"Lovey, we insisted on it. Your mother wouldn't be able to sleep otherwise."

How had her entire life been so completely turned upside down?

"They're fetching us to board the plane. We love you, Liss."

They each said a quick goodbye, promised to talk again soon, and then she was left staring at a blank screen on her phone.

Still as restless as she had been, she dialed Joseph, who was covering for her.

"I'm already at the pub so Mary can update me on new procedures. Wanted to spend a couple of hours with her while I reorient."

"Good idea."

"Everything's under control, and yes, I promise I'll call if I need you."

Talking to him made her feel as if she were doing something useful, even though she hadn't been needed at all. Others seemed to be handling all the pieces of her life, which meant she had the time she needed to work on her graphic arts project.

After showering then dressing in jeans and a long-sleeved shirt, she searched out Jacob. She knocked on the door where she'd previously found him, and when there was no answer, she called out his name and reached for the handle.

A red light on the wall next to the door blinked, and she noticed a small touchpad there. When she placed a fingertip against it, a buzzer blasted, the sharpness ricocheting around her and making her jump back.

More surprises.

She went downstairs and, when she didn't find him, continued toward his wing of the house. "Jacob?"

"Back here!"

Near his bedroom, one of the doors stood ajar.

Still, before crossing the threshold, she knocked.

"Enter."

When she did, he turned his chair toward her. His smile was inviting, sending another little tingle through her.

"I... Uh." She tucked hair behind her ear. "I didn't realize you had two offices."

"The other is more for cameras. In an emergency, it doubles as a panic room."

"Hence the door on it?"

"Actually you'll find that type of lock in several places in the house. Anywhere I might require privacy."

"The room you don't want me to see?" Why had she blurted that out? "Unless you were joking about having one."

"No. I assure you I wasn't."

Fear collided with excitement and turned her tummy upside down.

"And yes, it's protected...with biometrics. Do you want to see it?"

"Absolutely not." *Yes. Desperately.*

His grin was quick, evil. "So there's something else I can do for you?"

He twitterpated her so much she had to shake her head to remember why she'd sought him out. "I need to do some work. So if the offer of using the garage apartment is still open, I'd like to take you up on it." Having separate spaces was more important now than it had been an hour ago. After his teasing invitation, she'd never be able to think as long as they were under the same roof.

"I'll walk you over."

She hurried back to the living room ahead of him so their bodies didn't come into close proximity. And then she followed him out the sliding glass patio door and across to the former barn.

The upstairs space blew her away. It wasn't a tiny office—it was more like an artist's studio, with wide-open spaces and massive windows that allowed plenty of sunlight. The honey-colored wood floors were divine. There was a comfortable-looking couch, a daybed, and an anti-gravity gaming chair behind an L-shaped desk that offered her more workspace than she'd ever enjoyed before. "This is as big as my apartment."

"You're pleased?"

"It's spectacular. Really. The views..." The windows were massive, and he'd been right about the natural light that filtered in.

"There's an attached deck, through that door. Make yourself comfortable while I bring over the computer."

After he left, she took his advice and explored her temporary work area. There was a small powder room and a tiny kitchenette, complete with a small refrigerator that was stocked with water bottles and splits of champagne. This apartment couldn't be any more perfect for her.

Then she walked out onto the small deck. It was only big enough for a bistro set and a single Adirondack chair, but it overlooked the meadow and Saddle Mountain. It was a perfect place to escape with a cup of tea or an evening sip of bubbly.

Jacob returned with the box containing a sleek, space-agey titanium-encased tower. It was not just functional, but a work of art with the company's famous curved lines.

Awed, she trailed her fingers down the side. "I've never seen anything this beautiful."

"Not sure I have either. I'm told it's next year's Elite Pro model. And it's been upgraded with an additional twenty thousand dollars' worth of graphics cards."

"I'm..." *Speechless.* This was the stuff of dreams. She couldn't afford the base model, let alone the upgraded pro one. "Wow."

"Apparently Bonds said that you'd appreciate something this..." He cleared his throat.

Elissa waited.

"Sensuous."

Heat seared her cheeks. The mysterious Julien Bonds knew far too much about her. "He said that? Or are you making it up?"

"I assure you—sensuous is not a word I would have associated with a computer." He tucked the unit beneath the desk. "The monitor is significantly bigger."

"Do you need help?"

"You can hold the doors."

A few minutes later, in the apartment, he opened the box.

Even though he was a big, muscular man, the thing was massive.

"Bonds included these." He handed her two smaller packages with her name on them, then read the enclosed note aloud. "Gadgets he thought you'd enjoy."

"This is like Christmas." Only better. She opened the first gift. "Oh my God. Drool-worthy."

"What is it?"

"Pen tablet."

"That means something to you?"

"I can draw free hand on the pad, and the image will appear on the screen. It's a much better quality than the one I already have."

"And the other thing?"

She tore open the gift and blinked. "It's an editing console, which means I don't need a mouse or keyboard to manipulate images." With her right hand, she showed him the wheels and buttons. "For example, this one is for contrast. No clicking on anything separate."

"Time saver?"

"Huge." It was impossible to believe that Julien Bonds had put all of this together for her.

Jacob placed the monitor stand on the desk. "Want to give me a hand with the screen?"

He sliced through the cardboard with a pocketknife, and then she jiggled the foam packaging loose.

Once she caught a glimpse of the frameless monitor, she gasped. "I've only seen things like this in museum displays and when I've watched videos of the big electronics show." It took both of them to secure it in place. "I'm just flabbergasted." The screen was at least fifty-five inches. "It weighs a ton."

"Sixty pounds or thereabouts."

Within minutes, he had the entire thing put together and connected to the internet.

The Bonds logo winked into view in the middle of the see-through glass, and the crispness took her breath away. "This is unbelievable."

"The tag says it displays over a billion colors."

"That shouldn't even be possible." She wrapped her arms around herself. "I can't believe I get to work on this." But she was afraid she'd never want to give it up when she returned to her real life. Even monthly payments on this would be equal to a car. "I'll leave you to enjoy your new toy." After pointing out where panic buttons were located, Jacob programmed his phone number into her new cell phone. "As I stated earlier, there are agents on the property. I have one stationed at the gate, and two on perimeter patrol. However, you're not likely to see them. Anything else?"

"I think this more than covers it. I couldn't be happier. I mean, you know…"

"Given the situation?"

"I don't want to sound ungrateful."

"Being at a safe house is always an adjustment."

And that was exactly what this was. "Thank you. Not for bringing me here, but for—"

He held up a hand. "Let's leave it at thank you. And you're welcome." With a curt, dismissive nod, he excused himself.

She paced to the window and watched him until he closed the patio door behind him.

For the first half hour, she played with the computer, learning her way around before opening her design program, then clicking on the icon for her client's collateral.

After making a few adjustments, she let her mind wander.

The new machine—combined with the surroundings—should have been enough to inspire her for weeks. Yet she couldn't concentrate.

Elissa grabbed a bottle of water from the tiny refrigerator. A loud whinny captured her attention, and she paced to the window. Seconds later, Jacob rode into view on horseback, tall in the saddle, wearing a cowboy hat. Even though he was far away, there was no mistaking the rope attached to the saddle.

Again, unbidden, his soft threat from the night before teased the edges of her memory.

He continued on, and soon two other men galloped toward him. When they were close, each rider pulled up and formed a semicircle. Because she wanted a better view, she went out onto the deck.

The impromptu meeting lasted for at least ten minutes, and she watched every moment, shamelessly drinking in the masculine and commanding sight of him. If only they'd met under other circumstances...

At an easy canter, the party loped away, toward the open valley. Without looking back toward her, Jacob lifted a hand in a silent acknowledgment.

He'd been aware of her the whole time?

She uncapped her bottle. Of course he knew exactly where she was. No doubt he had some sort of cell phone app that was streaming images of every part of the property.

When they disappeared over a hill, she went back inside, leaving the door open.

This time, when she sat back down at her desk, she was inspired, but not to work on the project that was due at the end of the week. Instead, she accessed one of her private folders, containing the images that Julien Bonds had called kinky shit.

He might be right. No doubt plenty of people would agree.

To her, though, it was more, a pure and honest expression of sensual pleasure.

In college, she'd taken all the art classes that were offered. As part of her final grade, she'd had to display her work at a small avant-garde gallery in Denver. Her drawing of a nude caught the eye of a Dominant who had then commissioned her to paint a portrait of his submissive.

When she'd arrived at their house for the initial interview, the Dom had outlined his expectations. It needed to capture emotion. While most of Lydia's body was to be bare, scarlet silk should cover her most private areas. He wanted to see just a hint of her nipples through the fabric—as if she were a precious gift to be unwrapped only by him.

And then he'd brought out heavy, thick silver chains.

Elissa had gasped at the sight. Until that moment, she'd known nothing about BDSM, and seeing the way Lydia glanced up at her Dominant with a soft smile rocked Elissa, expanding her view of the world.

Then, he'd nodded, and Lydia sank to her knees.

Belatedly Elissa grabbed her phone and snapped a dozen pictures of the sub, capturing her expression of adoring, blissful surrender.

During the weeks they worked together, Elissa received an education about Dominance, submission, what BDSM was, and what it wasn't.

The dynamic intrigued her enough to accept their invitation to attend an open house at a downtown Denver club and to eventually scene with a couple different Dominants.

Later, she'd entered that ill-fated relationship with Robby. It had taken months and endless conversations with other submissives to help Elissa realize that his need to manipulate her had nothing to do with actual Dominance.

For a while after that, she would only scene with one of the club's owners. Once she regained her bearings and learned to trust her newfound intuition, she moved on to other partners.

Because of her father's illness and the sheer number of hours she worked, Elissa hadn't been to the club since last summer. She'd missed it terribly—not just the connection with another person, but the sublime transcendence that occurred when she surrendered to an honorable Dominant.

Shoving aside the restlessness churning inside her, she opened one of her completed files and critically studied the image.

According to Hawkeye, Julien had suggested she show some of her work. She hated to disagree with a renowned genius, but clearly she didn't have enough talent. These images wouldn't be good enough even if she painted them as actual portraits—maybe because each subject reflected some part of her own personality.

Dismissing Julien's opinion as kind and nothing more, she minimized the image and opened one she'd been playing with for days.

In it, the submissive was kneeling back on her heels in front of a standing Dominant. Her head was bowed, and her dark hair fell over her face, shading her features. The backs of her hands rested lightly on her thighs. She wore a short gossamer gown, and a small collar circled her neck.

The man held a delicate chain, and he looked at his submissive with absolute adoration.

Elissa wrinkled her nose as she zoomed in on the Dom's features. Her intent was to show that he didn't need anything substantial to secure the woman's compliance. Their relationship was based on love and trust, respect, as well as consent.

The image wasn't quite what she wanted. Something was still missing.

Using the highly responsive mouse, she darkened the background to add a little more intensity. Then, still not satisfied, she changed the first layer entirely, making it dark gray so the submissive's gown appeared more ethereal.

Better.

But still not exactly what she was striving for.

Something about the man's facial features wasn't quite right. Maybe he needed to be a little more intense. With a few deft strokes, his jawline became more angular. Then she selected a deeper shade of green for his eyes.

Each alteration brought him into sharper relief, pleasing her.

Continuing on, she gave his abs slightly more definition before adding a small scar to his torso. She didn't want him to be perfect—she wanted him to be real, with flaws that made him human and gave him the capacity to care.

Then, satisfied, she enlarged the entire image to fill her screen.

In stunned fascination, she blinked.

The changes made her Dom resemble Jacob. *What in the hell?*

"Chardonnay?"

Screaming, heart pounding from sudden panic, she jumped.

"Didn't mean to frighten you."

Slowly, she spun her chair to face the door.

Jacob.

Late-afternoon sunshine silhouetting him, he stood in the entryway, holding an insulated tumbler that served as a wineglass. "I knocked. Dinner's close to being ready, and I thought you might want to unwind a bit first."

"I…" Somehow, she'd lost track of the hours. "That's thoughtful."

He stepped across the threshold and closed the door behind him.

Obviously he'd showered after his ride. The scent of summer wrapped around him, and his dark hair was still damp. He'd changed into a navy T-shirt and blue jeans. And it was everything she could do to pretend she wasn't turned on by him.

"Mind if I have a look at what you're working on?"

Horrified, she turned back to her computer to hide the image. But since the computer was slightly different from hers, the key she pushed didn't make the screen go blank.

He moved in behind her and looked at the screen over her shoulder. "That's..."

What? Had he noticed the Dom's resemblance to him? Or maybe the connection was only clear to her. She held her breath as she waited for him to speak.

"Is this what Bonds was talking about? The art he thinks should be in a gallery?"

Embarrassment raked through her, and she gave up on the lie that they were for a client. "This one is a rough draft." It shouldn't matter what the hell he thought, yet his opinion was important to her.

"It's stunning. And if you have others that are equally as good, I'm really impressed."

His warm approval sent shivers dancing up her spine.

"I'd like to have a look at all of them." His voice was soft with invitation.

She wasn't sure that was a good idea. Showing him would expose her in a way she'd never been before, making her vulnerable.

He waited in respectful silence.

Then, with a soft sigh, decision made, she opened another folder and selected the slideshow setting.

Each of her images appeared onscreen for a few seconds before vanishing.

When the final one faded and she clicked the mouse to exit, he took a step back, and she swiveled to face him.

"Bonds is right. They're spectacular."

She'd given Jacob her trust, and he'd honored it.

"You should consider it."

Her hand trembled as she accepted the chardonnay. "I have line drawings of course. But painting actual portraits? It's time-consuming, and that's something that's in short supply right now. Maybe after my parents get back from Ireland." And life returned to normal. Whatever that was. "And I'm not sure any gallery would actually display them."

"Why not?"

She scowled at him. Was he dense? "In case you haven't noticed, they're more than a little risqué."

"And tasteful. There's nothing overtly sexual. In fact, they're more intimate than anything."

Her mouth fell open a little at his observation. That was exactly what she'd been hoping to convey, but that he'd gotten it made her heart soar.

"That makes them perfect for collectors and lifestyle connoisseurs. I'm sure there are online options for sales as well."

"Honestly, I'd never considered it."

"If Bonds believes there's an opportunity, there is. Or he'll create one."

"I appreciate your feedback." She took a long, fortifying sip to cover her nerves and embarrassment.

"Are they inspired by real-life events?"

She choked on her wine. Of course he was curious. But wanting to avoid this type of prying question was one of the reasons she'd never shared her art. "Let's just say I have an active imagination."

"Do you now?" He tipped his head to the side—seeing through her half answer?

He didn't pursue his line of questions, which should have relieved her. Instead, disappointment churned through her. For the first time in over a year, she wanted to be pushed.

Jacob appealed to her on so many levels, and every feminine instinct hummed with awareness. She longed to be in his arms, once again crumbling beneath the demand of his kisses.

"Is everything okay?"

"Fine." She shook her head to vanquish her absurd thoughts. "Yes. Of course. Why?"

"Do you have any experience?"

"Uhm…" He couldn't possibly mean what she thought he did. *Could he?* "With?"

"BDSM."

Her pulse skittered to a stop before racing on frantically. Maybe she wasn't ready for this after all.

As if he had all the time and patience in the world, he widened his stance, then folded his arms across his chest and regarded her.

His actions were so perfectly Dominant that instinctive arousal crashed through her.

The silence dragged while she squirmed.

As she'd guessed, this man knew exactly who she was, what her needs were. If she wanted, she could change the subject or refuse to answer. Or she could take a chance and see where things went. With a nervous sigh, she told him the truth. "Yes. I have some experience."

"And are you planning to ask me to give you what you want?"

Her tummy plunged into a terrifying freefall. "I'm…" Heaven save her from this man and the way he so perfectly read her. "I'm not sure what you mean."

"No? I think maybe you're deflecting, Elissa. And when you're ready, it's safe to tell me the truth about who you are."

CHAPTER FOUR

HAWKEYE

Jacob was taking a gamble. A big fucking one. But the military and life-and-death black ops situations had honed his instincts and taught him to respect his hunches.

And the beautiful woman with wide, unblinking eyes and with her mouth slightly parted in shock was a submissive. Even if instinct hadn't told him that, her stunning art would have.

Elissa was capable and resourceful, no doubt. Strong enough to live her life on her own terms. While he was at her family's pub, he'd studied her. She managed the place well, took care of the customers, and had been polite but direct when she told him it was time to leave. And then, outside, she'd been resolute in her determination not to go with him.

In addition to being attracted to her, he respected her. And there was no mistaking the fact that the male subject in the image she was working on resembled him.

The kiss last night had proven that she was interested in him. The question was, what were they going to do about it? He wasn't inclined to ignore it, but getting involved with a client was beyond stupid. He didn't take unnecessary risks. Or hadn't, until now. Elissa was no ordinary woman, and he'd never had a reaction to a woman like he did to her.

He continued to wait, wondering if she'd go on. If she didn't, that was answer enough, and he would respect her boundary.

The next move was hers entirely.

"You've already seen more than most people." Ambiguity hedged her response, and she knitted her fingers together around her glass, maybe to disguise her nervousness.

"I appreciate your belief in me." There was no gift more valuable.

"But for me, I guess the question is, who are you, Jacob? Beyond someone Hawkeye trusts with my life? A man who lives far away from the world, in his own private fortress? Someone who gets what he wants?" She tilted her head back to look up at him.

On some level, the fact she remained where she was and he stood so near, towering over her, was the first step in the dance that might culminate in a D/s experience. "Are you asking if I understand what I'd need to do to satisfy your need to submit?"

Her breath whooshed out, and her face turned a charming shade of scarlet. There was no artifice about her. Because of the life he'd lived, he appreciated that as much as a cool summer breeze. Jacob couldn't get enough of her.

"That's not exactly what I meant. I wouldn't have put it in those words."

"So how would you have put it?"

"I wanted to know about you and your experience."

It was a fair question. "On some level, I was always aware that I was a Dominant. When I was in college, I attended a club in New Orleans and mentored under the owner. Once I'd explored the dynamic, I understood why none of my attempts at dating had progressed into something more permanent. The most important thing about BDSM is the amount of honesty it requires." He studied her expression as he raised an eyebrow.

Clutching her glass even tighter, Elissa nodded.

"Would you like me to be blunt?" He waited for her nod before going on. "I think I'm right about you." He shrugged. "But that's for you to admit when you're ready. I'm interested in pursuing this conversation—and you—but only if you're willing."

"That's..." She took a sip of her wine. For courage? "You're definitely direct."

"As honest as I can be. You deserve that. So whether you tell me I'm wrong and we pretend this—and your reaction to my kiss last night—never happened is totally up to you."

"You're not wrong, but I wasn't expecting this. It feels a bit surreal."

Her soft admission meant a lot to him, but they would proceed at her pace. "We can always address this again at another time."

The wine sloshed gently against the sides of the glass, telling him her hands were shaking.

Hoping to take away some of her tension, he crossed the room and returned with a chair, then took a seat across from her. It brought them closer together, inviting trust rather than creating a disparity.

"So everything with you is safe, sane, and consensual?"

He studied her. "Of course." While he knew plenty of people who embraced RACK—Risk Aware Consensual Kink—he hadn't had a relationship that had ever developed that far. He understood the appeal. And perhaps with the right partner and enough time, he was open to the possibility. As it was, he continually communicated with his submissive to ensure her comfort and pleasure.

"Without emotional manipulation?"

What the fuck? He scowled. But when he spoke, he kept his voice low. "Is there something I need to know?"

"Look..." She stood and slid her tumbler on the desk before striding to the window. A few seconds later, she turned to face him. "Maybe I'm not ready for this. Can we have this conversation somewhere else? Maybe a bit later?"

"Whenever you're ready."

"Maybe after dinner?"

"I'm cooking." He shrugged. "The one thing that's my specialty."

She gave him a small smile that told him she appreciated the reprieve. "I'll be over in a while, after I shut down my computer and straighten my desk."

"Take your time."

Forcing himself to push away thoughts of a relationship with Elissa, he strolled back to the main house, automatically scanning the area to be sure everything was quiet. So far, there'd been no reports of unusual activity on the ranch. An hour ago, he'd checked in with Hawkeye. There'd been no further attacks that the firm knew of. No one was relaxing their vigilance, but it was possible the anthrax sent to Inamorata had been an isolated incident.

Even if it was, that person needed to be found.

As he seasoned steaks, images of Elissa, and her art, filtered through his brain. And he remained enthralled by the one she'd been working on. She'd done an excellent job of capturing the Dominant's features. There was appreciation in his eyes, and he wondered if she'd seen something similar in his.

When she finally entered through the sliding glass door, he looked across at her. There was nothing more perfect. Like she belonged. A future with moments like this would work for him.

"Hey." She slid her glass onto the counter.

"Steaks okay?"

"From your cattle?"

"And dry aged. Nothing but the best." Earlier, while she was working, he'd tossed a salad and baked some potatoes. "There's a bottle of red wine on the island. I took it out of the fridge earlier to reach room temperature. Will you grab it?"

Only their second meal together, and already they were working like a team.

"Merlot?"

"Do you like it?"

"One of my favorites. Not too heavy." After she handed the bottle to him, he uncorked it and poured them each a glass.

Once again, they agreed to eat outside, and she set the table while he fired up the grill.

When he joined her, she took a small breath, and for a moment he thought she was going to say something. But with a tiny shake of her head, she settled for thanking him.

As they dined, he decided to follow her lead. If she chose not to mention their previous conversation, he would honor that. And when she asked about his upbringing on the ranch, he ended up revealing more about his family history than he'd ever told anyone. "I mentioned my mother already. She was an only child and hated living out here. Right after she graduated from high school, she moved to Los Angeles."

"Bright lights. Big city."

"She got pregnant in her early twenties and moved back home. I never knew my father."

"That has to be tough."

He shrugged. "My grandparents did the best they could. I didn't make it easy for them. Something I'll always regret."

"And your mom. Where is she now? Still in California?"

"I'm not sure." The answer was much more complicated

than that. The truth was, he didn't know. Hawkeye had gotten her out of the hellhole that was her life in Mexico. She hadn't thanked him for the help and was furious when Jacob pulled strings to have her admitted to rehab. After a few days, she'd checked herself out and disappeared.

With Hawkeye's vast resources, there was no doubt Jacob could locate her. But she'd made it clear she didn't want to be found. "She has problems with addiction."

"I didn't mean to pry."

He wanted to know her deepest secrets. Fair was fair. "I was two or three when she left for the second time. Said the stress of dealing with a kid was too much."

"I'm sorry." Elissa placed her fingers on the back of his hand. The touch was both gentle and reassuring. And he absently wondered how long it had been since he'd experienced either. Odd. Until this moment, he hadn't missed it. And now the need for connection blasted through him like the roar of a freight train. "She abandoned you?"

"You could say that. Or that she did what she thought was best for me. Or what she needed in order to save herself."

"That's generous of you."

"Is it? Would it have been better for her to live a life she hated?"

"Did she ever come back?"

"Never. When I was little, she made an occasional attempt to stay in touch. She called a couple of times and sent birthday cards often enough that I'd be excited to get another the next year. I'd check the mailbox several times a day for weeks, looking. Hoping." His grandmother would give him a slight smile, but there'd be pain in her eyes when she saw his disappointment. "I gave up when I turned nine."

Elissa winced.

For a long time, neither spoke. Then, seeming to realize how intimate her touch was, she drew her hand away.

"My grandparents did the best they could. And they were both great people. Grandad insisted I go to college so I'd be ready to inherit the ranch. At eighteen, I saw that as a curse. And maybe I have a bit of my mom in me. I wanted to see the world. There had to be something beyond these fenced-in acres. They worked from sunup to dusk and rarely took vacations. I couldn't imagine that for the rest of my life. So after I got my degree, I joined the military instead of coming home and repaying everything they'd done for me."

"I get it. Family expectations are complicated."

As he expected, she was compassionate rather than judgmental. Maybe she understood because of the way she ran her family's business.

"They didn't tell me Grandad was sick, or that they needed money because of the downturn in beef prices. They got behind on some of their loans and had to sell off parts of their holdings. Which is why I went to work for Hawkeye." The pay was beyond anything he'd imagined. It wasn't for the love of black ops. It was for the opportunity to redeem his selfish mistakes. "I wasn't there when he died. And my grandmother had to manage everything herself." Regret was his constant companion.

"You were young."

"Every day I'm grateful for what I have." In the military, he'd seen things that would haunt him forever. While working for Hawkeye, he'd done things that would haunt him forever. The world was big—that was true. But home was where he'd healed. He'd been there for his grandmother and continued the Walker legacy. "The connection with the land, the responsibility..." He glanced at Saddle Mountain, then back at Elissa with her beautiful, soulful eyes. "I've recognized it for what it is. A privilege, rather than a burden. But it's not for everyone. It can be lonely, and the winters are long."

"There are trade-offs, though. Right? The peace. I've been really creative out here." She looked into the distance for a moment. "I know you don't work for Hawkeye anymore. But it seems like a part of you. Like the biometrics and the panic room. Normal people don't live like that."

"No?"

"You mentioned the loneliness. Is there part of you that misses being an agent?"

"I've chosen to live in the present. I told him to fuck off when he first approached me about this job."

She traced a bead of condensation as it wended its way down the side of her glass. "Then why am I here? Why did you change your mind?"

"He showed me a picture of you."

She stilled.

"There was no way I could say no."

"And why the name Operation Wildflower?"

It'd been fanciful, maybe. But it fit. "Your eyes." He took a drink of his merlot. "Reminded me of columbines. They were my grandmother's favorite. I'd pick them for her, and she always pretended they were the greatest gift ever."

"My mom was the same with dandelions." She grinned. "But when you think about it, it means we wanted to give them a gift, and when you have no money, what else do you do?"

He liked the way she saw the world.

The sun moved toward the horizon, and she shivered.

"We can clean up here, then finish our wine near the firepit while we watch the sun set."

"That sounds perfect."

Within minutes, their chores were done, and they were back outside. He held a lighter to the kindling. It caught almost right away, and a soft crackle filled the air.

He sat on one end of the couch, and she curled up at the other beneath a blanket he'd carried out for her.

The first hint of orange brushed the high, wispy clouds.

"It's impossibly quiet out here." She took a sip of her wine.

"You're happy in the city?"

"To be honest, I've never really thought about it. It never occurred to me to move away from my parents. I went to college, got my own place, but my parents and the pub mean the world to me."

"The constant movement."

"It's electric in a way, never silent. Kids playing. People coming and going at all hours—myself included. Parties. Even noise from televisions. But this…"

"I've grown accustomed to it. You can hear the world in a whole new way. The birds. The wind in the trees."

"Horses neighing."

"You were watching."

"I couldn't help myself."

It was an intimate confession, one he didn't respond to, choosing instead to allow the time to unfurl as she wanted.

"You had a rope on the saddle."

Jason hid his grin behind his glass. "I know how to use it."

As usual Waffle appeared from nowhere, leaping onto the couch, to land between them. She head-butted Jacob's leg before plopping down to clean herself.

"Where does she go?"

"She patrols the property, and she has a pet door entrance into the garage. She has a bed, and when it gets cold, I have a heat lamp to keep her warm." He stroked the feline's head. "We haven't had a single issue with mice or skunks since she took up residence. Even the raccoons seem to have packed up their babies and moved somewhere else."

"She earns her keep."

For a few minutes, Elissa watched as the sun sank behind

Saddle Mountain. Then she faced him and took a deep breath. "Have you ever had a submissive?"

Though the question didn't surprise him, her directness did. "As in a twenty-four-seven relationship?" When she nodded, he answered. "No." Guessing she was looking for a more detailed answer, he examined his own motivation, maybe for the first time. "My lifestyle has never been conducive to that kind of commitment. In the military, I was Special Forces, and I deployed a lot." He shrugged. "Then after Peru—"

"So you *were* there."

He didn't acknowledge her statement. "I went to work for Hawkeye. Then when we nearly lost the ranch, I knew I needed to be here for my grandmother. She deserved that."

She propped a pillow behind herself, bringing her a little closer to him. "You're a good man."

"I've done some things I'm not proud of. Bad things."

"All of us have regrets."

Some were easier to live with.

The fire crackled and hissed, and the automatic outdoor lights turned on. They weren't bright—rather they provided enough illumination to add ambience and safely maneuver around.

He'd enjoyed the patio more since she arrived than he had in the past few years. Though she hadn't been here long, she was already affecting his life.

Last night, it had taken him over an hour to fall asleep. He'd told himself it was because he heard every one of Elissa's movements and was concerned for her safety. But the truth was so much more.

As a man, as a Dominant, he noticed everything about her —feminine curves, rumpled hair, feisty attitude, talent, loyalty to her family, even her unintentional submissive air.

It'd been years since he had such an intense reaction to

any woman. He'd taken a shower and jacked off while he was in there. Since that hadn't helped much, he'd masturbated a second time. The rest he eventually managed to get was light and fitful.

When he didn't go on, she placed her glass on the wicker table. "So you're not much for relationships?"

He hadn't been.

When he didn't respond, she went on. "I think they give our lives meaning."

Jacob had few friends, even fewer close ones. Maybe he was missing out.

"Have you thought about kids? Having someone to pass the ranch down to?"

"My grandparents want the land to stay in the family." But managing the holdings was a hell of an obligation, and developers had offered a lot of money for the property.

He could have a nice life somewhere else, debt free, with no responsibilities. Despite the temptation, he'd never been able to sign the papers. The work was meaningful, offering him satisfaction that couldn't be bought. And he knew his forebearers had struggled and sacrificed. It didn't seem right to turn his back.

She wrapped the blanket a little tighter around herself, and he stood to toss another couple of logs on the fire.

"What about you? As far as relationships?"

For a moment, she studied the crackling fire, as if deciding how much to reveal. "My first paying commission as an artist was from a Dominant. And that was my introduction to the lifestyle. Before we got started, both he and his submissive gave me an education. We talked about their relationship. I guess the biggest surprise for me was that they each said they received more than they gave."

He sat back down, a little closer to her than earlier, and she didn't scoot away.

"I loved being around them. It seemed as if they had their own form of communication. There was a reverence to it that I'd never seen before."

While he hadn't experienced anything like that, he, too, had witnessed it.

"I wanted something similar and was naive enough to think it was automatically part of a committed D/s relationship. You know, as if something magical happens the moment you agree to wear a Dominant's collar." She tipped her head back and stared at the moon for a long time.

Was she talking about one of her relationships? Despite an impatience that was uncustomary for him, Jacob remained silent, allowing her the space to sort through what she wanted to say.

"His name was Robby."

"Go on."

She wiggled around until she was facing him. "I met him at the club, and a couple of months later, I moved in to his apartment."

Undoubtedly she'd left a lot out.

"It was a mistake. Maybe my worst. He had rules about everything, and they changed continually. It got to the point I couldn't do anything right, and I was in trouble all the time." She looked away for a moment. "If I loved him, I'd try harder. Do better."

Anger flashed through him. She was special, to be protected and cared for. "Was it some sort of fucked-up punishment game with him?"

"Not necessarily. He was an expert at giving me the silent treatment and withholding sex and affection. He'd sleep in the guest room. Most times, he wouldn't tell me what I'd done wrong. He refused to attend my family's Christmas gathering. When I asked, he told me I knew what I'd done wrong. To this day, I still don't understand it." She shook her head and gave a helpless shrug that knocked him in the solar plexus. "His coldness would go on until I begged for forgiveness. And he never immediately granted it. I'd have to earn it a bit at a time. Cooking him special meals, sexual favors." She shifted, as if the confession had emotionally drained her. "I mean, that's part of BDSM—well, of any relationship, really. Right?"

"No." He shook his head. "There's a big difference. I get that no two relationships are the same, but there needs to be an agreement and reciprocity. Both partners need to get what they want. BDSM is not about one person's selfish need to be in control. And vanilla relationships should be the same way."

"That's what my mentors told me. It took an embarrassingly long time for me to really understand what was going on and to realize how to heal from it." She looked away for a moment.

When she refocused on him, she gave a small smile. "I guess that was my way of telling you that I don't date and that I confine my interactions to scenes at the club. And I haven't done that for a long time. Not since my dad got cancer, and I needed to take on more of their responsibilities at the pub."

He'd heard that from Hawkeye. But the pain that flitted through her eyes made Jacob's gut clench. He had an unusual —not entirely unwelcome—compulsion to soothe her.

Leaning forward, he reached for a wayward lock of her hair. "May I?"

"Uhm..." She held his gaze even as she drew in a shallow breath. "Yes."

His knuckles brushed the softness of her cheek as he tucked the strand back into place. He lowered his hand without touching her again. *Fuck.* The need to have her was a physical ache.

"Earlier, you said you were interested in pursuing me if I was willing." Her voice was the barest whisper.

He waited.

"I'm willing."

Around them, the entire night became preternaturally silent. He heard the sound of his own heartbeat. His cock hardened. He'd never wanted anything more. "Tell me what you're offering. Friendship? Sex? Or do you want to submit to me?"

Heat seared Elissa's lungs, and it was then she realized she was holding her breath.

Admitting she was interested in him was one thing. Telling him what she really wanted was terrifying.

At the club, the Doms were vetted. And she had been going there for so long that she knew most of them, at least by reputation. This, though, was entering uncharted territory. She trusted Jacob, but it had been so long since she'd been with someone new. Though attraction sizzled, she needed walls of protection around her vulnerabilities. "There would need to be rules, as well as a safe word."

He nodded, as she expected he would. "I wouldn't have it any other way."

"I'll go with red." She appreciated that he kept distance between them while they negotiated, but it would be so much easier to have the conversation if she were in his arms.

"And yellow for slow?"

"Yes."

"And your limits?"

"Because we haven't played together, I want to go slow."

He offered a quick, disarming grin. "Rope?"

Of course he'd remembered that from their earlier conversation. *"Yes."*

"Impact play?"

"Nothing too hard, at least for now." She shuddered, recalling a painful experience with Robby. "No canes or knife play, ever. Those are a hard limit. And nothing that would be permanent—I mean not that we'd have time for that, anyway."

"Agreed." He nodded. "Anything else?"

She shook her head. "If I'm gagged, I want to be sure I have a safe signal."

"Of course. As we discussed, safe, sane, consensual. I don't play dangerously, and I'd never put you at risk."

While he hadn't needed to say that, she was glad he had. It helped tamp down the tiny whispers of apprehension.

"And sex?"

Was she ready for that? The truth was, yes. She'd gone without a physical connection for so long that it consumed her. "As long as we use condoms." Robby had been awful about that. He hated the things, and he'd start with one on because she insisted, but sometimes he'd take it off during intercourse. Because of that, she ended up going on the Pill so he couldn't get her pregnant unless it was a joint decision.

In retrospect, that she'd even made that decision should have given her a clue that the relationship was in trouble. When he discovered what she'd done, fury had consumed him. He'd left for three days, and when he returned, he refused to have sex with her. Instead, he insisted on her servicing him. His anger burned for more than a month.

"And as for your rules?"

"We need to agree this is a temporary arrangement. Like we'd have at a club. It doesn't mean anything. When this is over, we'll walk away and forget each other."

"Sorry, Elissa." He shook his head. "I can't agree to that."

She scooted as far away from him as possible.

"You're not some random woman I can fuck and forget."

At his raw crudeness, she flinched.

"I'm sorry you're offended. But that's not how this works." He took a breath. When he continued, his tone was low, but his words were measured and uncompromising. "You matter to me, and you have since the moment I saw your picture. I can't dictate your emotions, and if you want to detach sex from your feelings, go ahead. But don't expect the same from me."

The force of his reaction stunned her. The men she played with were happy to scene and then go back to their regular lives. She hadn't expected him to be any different.

"Those are *my* terms." He paused to study her. "Now it's up to you. Do you still want to play?"

CHAPTER FIVE

HAWKEYE

Fighting for equilibrium, Elissa took a breath. She'd never really had to negotiate in this way before. Generally she told a Dominant what her limits were and informed him of her safe words. That there wouldn't be a relationship later was understood. At the end of the scene, they each went their own way.

Until now, she'd never had to be concerned with what her Dominant wanted. She was now navigating unfamiliar territory. "Can we agree that whatever we share stays here? Let's make no promises about what happens after this is over." Why did that thought cause a pang of grief? "It doesn't need to be complicated."

"Elissa, you were a complication before I met you."

She attempted a grin but then realized he wasn't joking. "I don't know what you want here."

"Every damn thing you have to offer. Hold nothing back. I want to hear your moans. Your whimpers. Your pleas. Your screams. And I fucking want to know I'm not some random Dominant who you'll forget next week."

After swallowing the sudden lump in her throat, she told him the truth. "I think you know better. Believe me when I say you're unforgettable."

"Good. Otherwise we'd be done here."

"We're getting somewhere." She exhaled a breath she hadn't realized she'd been holding. "So, can we at least agree that we'll part ways without looking back?"

"No."

"No?" She blinked.

"I respect your need for rules, but this isn't something I am flexible on. I'll always be honest with you—that's a promise. There will be no manipulation. But when the mission is over, if either of us want to discuss the possibility of continuing a relationship, we should be allowed to."

Maybe he was braver than she was. She wasn't sure she was ever capable of confessing her feelings like that. "But—"

"Maybe neither of us will want it. But I don't want to play guessing games with you. Can you at least attempt to be equally transparent with me? If you want me at the end of our time together, I need to hear it."

"I…" They were two different people from two different worlds who'd never chosen to be thrown together.

"Try."

The level of transparency he demanded was unlike anything she'd ever experienced. And it was as scary as hell.

"It's not that difficult."

Elissa always waited for a man to express his desire for a relationship first. At a club, she was different because a scene there didn't have the kind of meaning that one with Jacob would. "Terrifying."

"But you accept my terms."

Finally she nodded.

His smile was her greatest reward.

"And now… Would you like to submit to me?"

"Yes." Every part of her ached for what he offered. Without conscious thought she looked away, but then dug for courage. "I want you to dominate me, Jacob."

He placed his palms on the sides of her face and tipped her head back for a gentle kiss, one that conflicted with the untamed hunger burning in his eyes.

"In that case, Elissa…" He stood and offered his hand.

Her whole being trembled as she accepted, sliding her palm against his. The blanket tumbled to the ground as he drew her against him.

"I'll be worthy of your trust."

He released her to extinguish the fire and straighten the area, gathering their wineglasses.

"Now, like a good submissive, I want you to precede me into the house."

His voice contained an unfamiliar note of command. She was no longer a client, and he'd masterfully started the scene. Adrenaline flooded her, and she took a breath to steady the onslaught of nerves.

He nodded almost imperceptibly toward the house. Obediently, now on familiar footing, she walked across the patio and into the living room. Once there, she stood patiently, head bowed, trying not to fidget as she waited for him to lock the door and load the stemware into the dishwasher.

"Very nice."

The purr of his approval flowed through her, replacing nerves with confidence.

After engaging the alarm system, he crossed the room to stand in front of her. "I'm going to kiss you again."

"Yes." She met his eyes. "Please."

He hadn't said just how passionate he'd be. He tasted of

rich red wine, and he claimed her mouth like a man dying of thirst. Her surrender wasn't enough, and he plunged deeper, one palm pressed against the middle of her back and the other cradling her head as he coaxed a response from her. He wasn't allowing her to be passive—he demanded her active participation.

At the club, no Dominant had kissed her.

Once again, Jacob proved he was no ordinary man.

He pulled away for a moment. Reeling, she blinked as she looked up at him. "Open your mouth wider for me."

When he'd said he wanted everything she had to offer, he meant it. She leaned against him, curling her hands around his neck as he devoured her.

By the time he eased back, her breathing was ragged, and the world was unsteady. He continued to hold her close; then he gently tipped back her chin.

"You're exquisite."

Ordinarily a compliment like that might have embarrassed her, but the sincerity radiating from his eyes spoke of authenticity. From him, it wasn't some meaningless platitude.

"Now I'd like you to follow me."

She nodded. Already she would follow him anywhere.

"I'd prefer to hear your answer aloud, please."

"Yes…" For a moment, she paused and frowned. "How should I address you?"

"Thank you for asking. Sir or Jacob. I'm fine with either."

"In that case, yes, Jacob."

"I like the sound of my name on your lips." He removed his finger from beneath her chin.

Quickly and effectively, he'd established a boundary, and she slipped a little deeper inside herself, to a place where the noise stopped. Sometimes that didn't happen until later in a scene, after impact play had begun.

He led the way to his wing of the house and stopped outside the closed door that she'd noticed last night.

"Is this the room you were talking about? The one you said I wouldn't like?"

"My dungeon? Yes." He flashed a quick, wicked grin. "At this point, I'm thinking you'll find it to your satisfaction." After the biometrics disengaged the lock, he turned the knob, pushed open the door, then turned on the lights before looking at her.

Giving me a chance to change my mind?

"After you."

Wanting this, wanting him, she entered slowly, then turned in a slow circle, taking in the space. It was a submissive's dream, with lots of mirrors, a spanking bench with lots of rings, as well as siderails for her knees, a rather large, uncomfortable-looking straight-back leather chair fit for a Dominant, and a beautiful wood Saint Andrew's cross with a small vinyl pad in the middle to make it more comfortable. That, she would appreciate. But what captured her attention was a metal structure. It had two upright poles and another that went across the top. It made her think of a high bar used for gymnastics.

Although there was no window, there was a sink, an armoire emblazoned with the ranch symbol, and a second door, maybe to a closet. There was a fireplace with a chair and rug in front of it, along with several sturdy metal rings attached to the floor…which no doubt meant he could secure her at his feet, something she'd never experienced before. "This is…"

"Frightening? Enticing?"

She faced him.

Jacob stood with his legs wide, arms folded across his chest, all commanding and ominous. His eyes were darker than they had been earlier, and while he still looked at her with kindness, there was now a glint of hardness in the green depths. In his element, he was magnificent. And he was studying her closely, waiting for her answer. It was difficult to express what was happening inside her, the collision of nerves and excitement. "Both, maybe."

"What scares you?"

"The rings in the floor."

"Interesting. Why?"

"The helplessness of it." With other Doms, it had been enough to say she didn't like something. But Jacob forced her to look inside herself. "And not knowing how long I'd be there. Would I be kneeling? Sitting? Lying down? Standing?"

"Go on."

She glanced toward the fireplace setting. "But that speaks to… I don't know how to put it into words. Like, I guess, a long comfortable evening between a Dom and a submissive. He—you—might be sipping a whiskey…"

"You remembered."

"To me it represents something permanent. It seems like something that might happen in a long-term relationship—you know, between a couple who spend a lot of time enjoying each other."

"I can see that."

"A scene kind of has a natural progression—a beginning, an end—and that can be thirty minutes or a couple of hours. But you go back to your life, cooking dinner, doing the laundry."

He waited, not saying anything.

"I'm not sure I have the patience to be tethered at my Master's feet." Had she really used the word Master? Something inside her stilled. She'd never had that thought about any Dominant, even the one she'd lived with. So why Jacob?

Her breaths were frantic as she fought to control her suddenly erratic emotions. "You've got this amazing setup.

Did you put it together for someone in particular?" It shouldn't matter, but she couldn't contain her curiosity.

"I have particular tastes. But no. You are the only woman—submissive or not—who has spent time in my house."

She took that in, loving that she was the first.

"I worked with a furniture designer in Denver to put the dungeon together. The cross is made with lumber from the ranch."

"It's beautiful, and I understand why you have that and the spanking bench. But I'm curious about the rings attached to the floor. Was my guess right?"

"I enjoy the flexibility they offer. And standing over a submissive who's helpless beneath me is a powerful image. For example, you could be on all fours, secured by a collar around your beautiful neck."

Unable to help herself, she pressed her palm to her chest.

"There'd be no escape as I eased a butt plug inside your ass."

His focus was relentless, and beneath his scrutiny, her pussy moistened. And he was still several feet away from her.

"You'd have no choice but to take my cock in your hot pussy as I entered you from behind." He took a step toward her, his footfall ominous on the honeyed floor planks. "You'd be full for me. And I'd show you no mercy."

Protective instincts urged her to flee, but submissive ones compelled her to stay rooted in place.

"Or maybe I'd place you on your back and require you to tug on your nipples as I dropped hot wax onto your belly."

Her knees were weak. It wasn't just from his words, but the intent beneath them. They were more than random musings. He was watching her, weighing her response.

"But I definitely like your idea—of seeing you tied at my feet while I sip whiskey in front of the fire."

Earlier, she might have put that on her limits list. But she was no longer certain of that. His scenario sounded companionable, emotional rather than sexual, and she suddenly craved that connection in a way she never had before.

"Do you know what would make this even more spectacular?"

"No." Tipping her head to one side, she looked at him. "What?"

"The image you're working on. Having the original portrait hanging on the wall above the mantel."

"Are you serious?"

"I'd like to commission the piece, if it's not too late."

Her mind reeled. *He wants it for himself?*

"Do you take requests?"

"I'm not sure what you mean."

"I'd like the submissive to have darker hair. Perhaps blue eyes as well."

He *had* seen his resemblance in the image, and he wanted the woman to look more like her? "I've never done something like that before." Of course, until today, she'd never changed an image to look like a man who was consuming her thoughts.

"Bonds recognized your talent. So do I. I'd like to purchase your art before you have a showing and the price goes up."

She laughed at the absurdity.

"I'll consider it an investment."

"Look, if you really mean it, I'll paint it and give it to you. I wouldn't feel right charging you."

"I insist. A lot of labor goes into it, not to mention supplies and the opportunity cost."

He was a businessman. Of course he'd understand that concept. While she was working on his piece, she couldn't earn money doing anything else.

Jacob named a price that made her gasp. It was twenty

times anything she'd consider charging. "I want the original, along with any line drawings. No posters, giclées, or any other reproduction. It's for my private collection, and no one else can ever see it."

The offer was absurd.

There was little chance she'd ever become famous. If she wanted to pursue a career as an artist, the picture would be a crucial part of her portfolio. And being able to make copies of it would be an ongoing source of income.

Yet no one else would ever have the connection to the painting that he did, and she'd always remember his belief in her—misplaced though it may be. *"If* I finish it, it's yours. And I agree to your terms. The price doesn't include framing or potential shipping charges."

"If you're not here when you complete it, simply name the time and place, and I'll personally pick it up."

"You could hire a professional company to do that."

"I know." The huskiness in his voice traced down her spine. "It's a deal, then?"

For better or worse. "Yes." Since this was a business transaction, she didn't add the honorific that would make her feel like his submissive.

He extended his hand.

"I said *if* I finish it," she reminded him.

"Hope is eternal, fair Elissa."

When she took his hand, he surprised her by raising hers to his lips. This badass protective agent, honorable cowboy, made her swoon.

She was falling for him, hard and fast.

When he finally released her, she looked away from him, trying to put some emotional distance between them. Her reaction had to be because of the strange circumstances, being alone with him in an idyllic setting and the millions of pheromones zinging between them, creating a bubbling cauldron of sexual need.

"You told me what scared you about the room." Like a good Dominant, he brought her back to the present, but he did so in a nonthreatening way that helped her to refocus. "What pleases you?"

This, a BDSM inquiry, was familiar and not as tricky to navigate. "The spanking bench."

"Tell me why."

"Depending on the position, it supports my whole body. It's comfortable. Because I can put my head down, I find it easier to let go mentally. It helps ease my worry."

"Good to know."

"I've never seen one of those in a club." She pointed to the metal structure.

"Let me show you how it works." He crossed the room, and she followed.

Now that she was close, she noticed the notches and hooks that were in it.

"It's a variation of a suspension frame. The height is adjustable, making it suitable for Shibari rope work. I have a different plan for it." Gently he moved her so she stood beneath the overhead bar. "Unlike the Saint Andrew's cross or the spanking bench, it allows unrestricted access to a submissive's body. Of course, she won't have the same kind of support as a more physical structure, so there are times, like a sustained, sensual flogging, where something else is a better choice."

Anticipation made her pussy damp.

"This frame allows the Dominant, me, to select a number of different positions for my sub—you."

She shivered.

"I can place you on your tiptoes. Or not." He never took his gaze from hers, and she was ensnared, helpless to look away. "Your ankles can be secured to the sides so that you can't escape or try to protect your pretty cunt."

The words hung in the still air, naked, frightening, tantalizing.

"Or I can bind your legs, in a mummy effect."

"It's..." *Words.* She needed to think. But how could she when he was mere inches away, talking about what he intended to do to her? "Ah...more versatile than I realized."

"The possibilities are numerous, aren't they?"

With her imagination painting some vivid pictures that she couldn't wait to sketch out, she looked away. Now that her creativity had been unleashed, she couldn't stop the flow of ideas.

"The metal plates at the bottom are bolted to the floor, giving the structure stability. That means you will be completely safe, and you're free to turn yourself over to me."

There was nothing she wanted more.

"Take off your shoes for me, Elissa." It was part invitation, part command, and his voice was as gruff as sandpaper over pebbles. "Then strip down to your bra and panties."

Though she'd expected the soft, uncompromising order, her heart still jolted. He was a new partner, and the unexpected was as wonderful as it was scary.

Her fingers trembled slightly, and she fumbled with the buttons on her shirt. She appreciated him walking away, toward the armoire, granting her a momentary reprieve from his focus.

Once she was half naked, her clothing folded on the floor, she tried to peek at what he was doing, but his back was to her, blocking her view.

He opened a drawer and placed a few items in it.

"Music?"

"I'd like that." Anything was better than the silence, amplifying the sound of her frantic breaths.

He selected something she recognized from the club, an EDM tune that pulsed with eroticism. "Do you like it?"

It made her more aware of him, of his constrained power. "Yes."

"I was hoping you would." He bumped up the volume a little more, giving the space an audible heartbeat.

"It's intimate. Moody."

"And not so loud that I can't hear your whimpers or cries of ecstasy." He glanced over his shoulder, and she wasn't sure whether or not he was joking.

Unsure what to do, she placed her hands at the small of her back and tried not to squirm as she waited for him.

When he faced her, he was holding a leather collar. "Any objection?"

The room held a slight chill, and she told herself her sudden shiver was from that.

"Elissa?" He'd obviously noticed her reaction. "Is it a problem for you?"

"I... Uhm..."

"It's your choice entirely."

In that instant, with the way he was looking at her, she was reminded of the couple she'd painted, the one she told him about.

The moment pulsed with expectation. To her, the collar represented some kind of commitment, but she wasn't sure he meant it that way. "Is it a fetish for you, Sir?"

"Not at all. To me, it's symbolic. It will be the only thing you'll have on, and from the moment I fasten it in place until I remove it at the end of our scene, it will mean you belong to me."

Being honest would make her emotionally vulnerable to him, yet she was compelled to confess what was in her heart. "I'd be honored."

"In that case, please lift your hair out of the way."

As she did so, he crossed the room. He placed a gentle kiss on her forehead, letting her know he appreciated her decision.

His touch both gentle and firm, he fastened the collar in place, then checked the fit. "Good." When she released her hair, he nodded his satisfaction. "You're mine." Possession punctuated his words. "It couldn't be more perfect if it had been custom-made for you."

Against her neck, the leather slowly warmed.

"Now finish undressing for me." This time, he watched, taking in her every movement.

When she was naked before him, she pressed her tongue to her upper lip. The club she played at had rules against nudity, and for a moment, uncertainty claimed her. She hadn't been this vulnerable since she was with Robby.

"You're even more spectacular than I dared hope." Jacob traced his thumb along the top of the collar.

Then, moving behind her, he cupped her breasts and dragged his thumbnails across her nipples.

Whimpering, she wrapped her hands around one of his wrists for support.

He leaned into her, his lips near her ear. "Do you like that, Elissa?"

She loved the way he whispered her name, the syllables laced with sensuality.

"Hmm?"

"Yes, I do. Sir."

He rewarded her by squeezing her nipples and gently tugging on them, with the right amount of exquisite pressure.

"And what do you think of floggers?"

"I love everything about them."

"Tell me."

She'd never had to explain it before, and she really hadn't

thought it through. "The way it bites. The way the falls can wrap around my body. So many points of contact. It's like a dance of pleasure and pain, and often both at the same time."

"Well said. And a violet wand?"

How could he expect her to think while he was tormenting her so exquisitely? "I've actually never played with one."

"Is it on your limits list?"

"No. I'm actually interested."

"Excellent." He released one nipple and skimmed his hand down her belly to find her heat. "Open your legs. *For me.* And keep them spread apart. Don't deny your Dominant."

Everything in her yielded to him.

He played with her pussy, teasing her to the very edge of an orgasm, and then he pulled away, leaving her shaking.

If she wasn't still holding on to him, she wasn't sure she could stand up. *"Jacob!"*

"Hmm?" He knew exactly what he was doing and seemed totally unconcerned. "Let's get you to the suspension structure so that you can earn that orgasm."

"You're such a damn Dom."

"Sounds like a complaint." This time, there was a hint of a tease in his voice, another new side of him.

Finding connection in a way she hadn't expected, she responded in kind. "It was more of an observation, Sir."

"An observation?"

"A proper submissive doesn't complain. She simply tries to please her Dominant."

"Exactly as I thought." He left her again and returned with a length of rope.

The sight of the sturdy bright-pink silk left her riveted. The color was arresting, and no doubt it would be the stuff of her future fantasies.

"Hold it for me."

She accepted the strand, and then he led her to the metal structure. Then, after studying her, he raised the top bar a couple of inches.

In less than a minute, her wrists were tied together and secured above her head. Fortunately he'd been kind and allowed her to keep her feet flat on the floor.

"Now spread your legs as far apart as possible."

With speed that attested to his skill with ropes, he had her completely at his mercy in no time at all. Nervousness crashed against her arousal, leaving her reeling.

He left her for a moment while he took out a metal box, then plugged in the violet wand and tucked the conduction pad inside the waistband of his jeans, which meant he didn't need the toy. He intended to use his body to electrify hers.

When he turned on the machine and tested it, the unmistakable sparking hum made her jump. She shrank back and tugged against her bonds. Not surprisingly, he hadn't left her much room to wiggle around.

"I have it on the lowest setting. Ready?"

For a moment, she considered using her safe word. But she told herself she could try it once. If she hated it, they wouldn't have to continue.

Opting for bravery, she nodded. "I'm a little apprehensive."

"Understood." He brushed two fingers between her breasts. "How's that?"

"Like...tiny bubbles." It was so light she was barely aware of it.

He touched both of her nipples, and absolute pleasure caused them to tighten immediately.

"Oh God. That's magnificent."

"Let's try a little more intensity."

When she didn't object, he adjusted the setting. This time,

when he skimmed her nipples, she cried out from pleasure. She never wanted this to stop.

Keeping contact with her, making her twitch from the little pulses, he moved behind her. He tormented her whole body—shoulders, breasts, ribs, belly. Determinedly he started over, from the top, trailing down her arms, then her sides, before zapping her buttocks, electrifying her.

Jacob crouched to electrify her legs, down to her ankles, before moving back up the insides of her thighs.

Instinctively she pulled away as he neared her most delicate spot, but the ropes caught, holding her prisoner. "Jacob…" She angled her head but couldn't make eye contact. "Sir?"

"Hmm?" But instead of stopping, he brushed his hand over her pussy.

The energy rocked through her. Instantly she became more aroused than she'd ever been. When he did it again, she whimpered. "I need…" God. She wanted sex. Had to have him.

But he was nowhere close to being finished with her.

When perspiration dotted her body, he left her only long enough to switch out the violet wand for a flogger with short falls. And he turned up the music, seeming to make the floor vibrate. Or maybe that was a residual effect of the electromagnetics.

For a few moments, Elissa allowed her eyes to close, and she was barely aware of his footsteps when he returned to stand behind her.

He swept her hair to one side and stroked a finger across her nape. "Are you doing okay, fair Elissa?"

She was. "Yes, Jacob."

"Ready for more?" He placed the strands of the flogger on her shoulder, then eased them back, igniting a promise of pleasure.

"I'm already in a submissive stupor."

"Good." He kissed the side of her neck. "Should we stop?"

"No." *Not ever.*

Her body chilled when he released her. Almost instantly he was in front of her, in all his Dominant magnificence. His powerful legs were spread, and he was still fully dressed, including his hand-tooled cowboy boots. Maybe she should have asked him to release her and take her to bed.

She expected him to begin the flogging, but he didn't. Instead, he pleasured her breasts and pussy until she writhed against him.

"I love seeing you so needy."

"May..." Damn, she wanted to come, but she knew he was finding pleasure in denying her. "I'm on the edge, Sir."

"Your eyes reveal all of your reactions. You can't hide anything." He lowered his hand. "Even your frustration. You'll come when I give you my permission."

She clamped her lips together so she didn't say anything else.

"Your brains match your beauty."

Then, taking a step back, he flicked the flogger across one of her breasts. She sighed. As a Dominant, he met her every need. She'd never been with a man who intuitively read her the way he did.

In total trust, she relaxed in her bonds, turning herself over to him.

Each thuddy stroke from the thick falls was everything she could have hoped for, the pain both blunt and welcome.

He was a master. Her Master.

She had no idea how long he kissed her body with the whip; all she knew was that she was lost in the reverberation of music, of whimpers. The tears clinging to her lashes were from happiness and release, and she was soaring, dancing in a place where only pleasure existed.

He placed the handle of the flogger against her clit and rubbed hard. When he spoke, his voice reached her from a distance, compelling and commanding. "Tell me what you want. Ask for it."

Over and over, he teased her, making her beg.

An eternity later, he yielded. "That's it. You've earned it. Come for me, fair Elissa. Come."

With a scream, she spiraled, letting go as the orgasm rocked her.

She rode wave after wave as he fucked her with his hand, wringing climax after climax from her, the last so intense that she tipped back, exhausted, with nothing left to give.

Jacob moved behind her to pull her body back against his. The steel of his erection pressed against her, making her woozy, delirious with desire.

Without her consciously being aware of it, he somehow managed to unfasten her wrists. "Wrap your arms around yourself."

Once she had enough awareness, she did. And then he rubbed her biceps, helping circulation to return.

Her entire body hummed with awareness.

As he released her ankles, he instructed her to close her legs when she was ready. After he stood, he captured her face between his palms. "Are you back with me?"

"Almost. I think." Her knees were still trembly. "That was..." Because her voice was little more than a whisper, she cleared her throat to try again. "Everything." She'd yielded to him in a way she never had with any other man.

"I need to get you some water, take care of you." He held her against his powerful body, and his heartbeat was steady beneath her ear.

She snuggled in closer, knowing something had been transformed inside her. She'd never be the same again. "Jacob..."

"Anything, Elissa."

God, she couldn't let this end. "Will you take me to bed? I want you to make love to me."

Her request stoked passion in his eyes. "There's nothing I'd like more."

CHAPTER SIX

HAWKEYE

Fucking hell.

In his thirtysomething years, Jacob had experienced more than some people did in a lifetime—he'd seen plenty of horrors that he wished he never had, and he'd left part of his soul back in a hellhole. But nothing—nothing—had ever affected him as deeply as seeing Elissa's beautiful tears while they scened. A part of his heart he believed long dead was slowly healing.

And now her lower lip trembled, as if she were uncertain of his reaction.

How was that even possible?

Though he was always a considerate lover and Dom, he'd never bonded with anyone like he did her. She was the perfect submissive, willing to try what he suggested and to trust him. She'd come apart in his arms, and then she'd turned to him for comfort. Not only was he honor bound to protect her, but now he was determined to find a way to keep her with him after the job ended.

Jacob swept her from the floor and carried her to his room, where he placed her on the bed.

The Dominant in him was tempted to tie her wrists to the headboard. But the need to have her arms around him while he made love to her overrode everything else.

"I've got to have you inside me."

He needed it more than his next breath.

After removing his boots, something he'd ask her—his beautiful little sub—to do in the future, he tugged off his T-shirt.

Elissa turned onto her side to watch him. He grinned.

"You're gorgeous, Sir."

Her voice was scratchy. With desire? "Not sure anyone has ever used that word in relation to me."

"They should have."

"You got the details right."

She frowned. "The details?"

"On the image you were working on."

"Oh my God. You saw?" An alluring shade of pink stained her cheeks. "It's not what you think. I mean…"

"I'm flattered. Thank you."

"Okay." She exhaled. "It wasn't intentional."

"I believe you." Neither of them were immune to the wild tug of untamed attraction. "But that's not why I bought it. There's an honesty about the piece. A yearning. A completion." And he'd think of tonight every time he looked at the finished portrait in his playroom. "I know you're wondering…" Jacob pointed to the raised bump on the far left side of his stomach. She'd replicated the jagged edges with extraordinary accuracy. And yet now, he saw the scar through new eyes. It was no longer just an ugly reminder of the past. Instead, it was a natural part of him, and a reminder that he was lucky. He'd gotten out alive. "It's from a knife." The wound had been deep, and the team medic had done his best to sew him together given the extraordinary circumstances.

"It means you survived. And we get this moment."

Jacob finished undressing, and she kept her focus on him. His cock was still hard, throbbing with insistent demand.

"You're…" She met his gaze. Throughout their scene, her eyes had become a darker shade of blue, and now they were wide. "Tell me you don't expect me to… I mean, you're massive!"

"Oh, Elissa, yes. I most certainly do." He generally didn't tease, but the indignation in her voice made it irresistible. "I expect everything from you. You're my submissive."

Frantically she shook her head.

"I've got a generous nature. We'll go slow." Then everything inside him became serious. He intended to claim her in every way possible.

Honoring her wish, he grabbed a condom from the nightstand drawer and rolled it down his length before joining her on the bed. "Part your legs for me."

"But I'm ready now."

"You'll be ready when I say you are. Now do as you're told before I get my ropes."

Interest sparked in her eyes. It wasn't defiance, but rather a revelation of what she craved.

"What'll it be?" He didn't have to ask the question. Every part of him knew the answer.

She set her chin in response.

His inner alpha happily responded in kind.

Jacob prowled to the closet to fetch his sturdiest rope. Unlike the silk he'd used earlier, this was sisal, a bit ragged, something he'd bought at the hardware store, suitable for use on the range. It might chafe, and at least for a little while, it would leave his mark on her body.

Impossibly, the idea made his cock even harder.

"Come to me, Elissa."

She didn't.

"Refusing to cooperate?" The more she played the game, the more ravenous he became. Whether she knew it or not, she was his.

Mine.

He'd used the word when he collared her earlier. He'd meant it, and this moment only reinforced his intention.

One way or another, Elissa Conroy was going to be his woman.

She curled into a ball, increasing the tension. He was going to fuck her so damn hard.

"Remember you asked for this," he reminded her as he picked her up and deposited her on the end of the bed.

When she immediately scooted back, he clamped on to one of her ankles and dragged her toward him. Her breath whooshed out, and her eyes darkened once more. She wanted things his way. She just wanted him to work for the victory.

Already he'd learned to recognize her expressions. He adored every aspect of her—playful, serious, emotional—and he vowed to fulfill all her fantasies.

Quickly he tied one of her ankles to prevent her from retreating again.

"Ouch! That stuff's rough!"

"Maybe that'll teach you to be a good sub and follow your Dominant's orders." *Lord, he hoped not.*

Once her other ankle was secure and she was spread before him, helpless, he crawled between her thighs, then parted her labia to devour her.

"Jacob! Don't." She thrashed her head. "I can't. It's too much."

"Would the lady like to wear a gag?"

"No!"

"In that case, I recommend you use your mouth for happy sounds. Moans, groans. Sighs. Or if you must, screaming my name." *That* would be the sweetest of all sounds.

"But—"

"Last chance." He slipped a finger inside her. "You're wet for me."

"Desperate for you."

He licked her clitoris rapidly, bringing her to the edge of an orgasm before slipping a second, then third finger inside to ensure she was fully prepared for him.

Her frantic cries were every bit as sexy as he imagined.

"Please." She curled her fingers into his hair and held him tightly. "I'm going to come."

This time, he wanted to own it.

Before she could climax, he worked his cock inside her welcoming warmth, a little bit at a time, letting her accommodate him.

"Oh…" She closed her eyes and thrashed her head from side to side.

"Yes. Take it."

Her pussy tightening around his cock, Elissa lifted her hips as much as her bonds allowed. *Fuck,* but she was so damn hot and tight.

He stroked harder and faster, meeting her demands.

When she screamed out her pleasure, he captured her mouth in a searing kiss, holding off his orgasm until she was completely satisfied.

Finally, she loosened her grip but didn't let go.

"That was spectacular, Sir."

"My pleasure, ma'am."

She smiled softly, then traced a fingertip across one of his eyebrows. "I've never experienced anything like that."

"Me either."

"Really?" She wrinkled her nose as she studied him. "Do you mean that? Or is it something you tell every woman?"

"Believe me when I tell you that I've never said it before. You're one of a kind, Elissa. And sex with you isn't like with anyone else." He began to move inside her again. Need was a raw and hungry thing, demanding completion.

"Come in me." Elissa met each thrust, concentrating all her energy on his pleasure.

Yeah. She was unique, all right. Perfect for him in every way.

Wanting her to always remember this moment, he took her deeply. With a guttural moan, he ejaculated in long, hot spurts. He'd wanted to claim her as his. But now he knew the truth. He was hers.

Breath ragged, mind splintered by his realization, he collapsed on top of her, then immediately rolled to the side so he didn't crush her.

"That was amazing." Fuck. He was a goner. This woman well and truly owned him. "*You* are amazing."

As confident as if she knew that already, she smiled.

He left the bed to release her ankles, and then he massaged them to restore circulation. "You've got a mild case of rope burn."

"I was hoping I would."

"My girl."

They agreed to shower together, and as they did, he inspected her body for marks. There were none from the flogger or the electroplay.

After lathering some gel, he washed her. He could live for the sound of her soft, sweet sighs and the way she swayed toward him.

Jacob took his time rinsing her off. "How was the violet wand?"

"Spectacular. All those sensations, everywhere. It's unlike anything else, and I'd enjoy playing with it again sometime."

"I also have attachments you might enjoy."

"Can I tell you something honestly? I liked that you used your body as the conduit. Your touch is what made it special."

"Anything my fair Elissa wants."

"Anything?" She curled her hand around his cock.

The whole time they'd been together in the shower, he'd become more and more aroused. And now, from her touch, he was fully erect.

She lowered herself to the tile floor and took him in her mouth and swirled her tongue around his tip, devilment dancing as she asked, "Even more sex?"

"Even more sex."

A few minutes later, they were dried off and back in bed. This time, they leisurely explored each other, and he savored every secret she revealed.

When it was over, he pulled her into his arms.

As she drifted off to sleep, she murmured something he couldn't quite make out. But she wiggled a little before settling more closely against his body.

He trailed a fingertip across her throat, then the collar he never wanted to remove.

Yeah, he'd seen a lot of ugly in his lifetime. Death. Despair. But Elissa's brightness was starting to vanquish the dark. For the first time in his life, he felt whole. And it was all thanks to her.

In gratitude, he kissed the top of her head.

"Good morning."

"Ugh. No." Elissa burrowed deeper under the covers and pulled the pillow over her head.

"I've got a surprise for you."

Next to her, the mattress dipped.

Jacob? Suddenly she was awake. Awake and scrambling to understand what was happening.

Images, memories, flashed through her mind. The violet wand. Calling him Sir. His hands on her. Him carrying her to his room and tying her to the bed before making sweet, sensual love to her. Then falling asleep—naked—in the comfort and protection of his arms.

He tossed the pillow aside, and she blinked a couple of times, bringing him into focus.

As always, he was breathtaking. Along with faded jeans, he wore a T-shirt that clung to his broad chest. The crisp scent of the outdoors clung to him, but it was his slow, predatory smile that sent cascades of shivers through her.

He was so complex, from stern—even implacable—to reassuring, sexy, and now this. Lethal. All at once, his smile made her remember yesterday while simultaneously hinting at what was to come today.

"I'm a smart man. I brought you tea. Duke Somebody or Other."

Smart? How about perfect? "I think you mean Earl Grey."

"Whoever. I watched you make it yesterday." He shrugged "Hope you like it."

She sat up, dragging the covers with her, conscious of her nudity. "Is there a reason for your...hospitality?"

"Other than wanting to please you?"

Elissa narrowed her eyes.

"And knowing you're not much of a morning person?"

"Or the fact you're taking your life into your hands by waking me up?"

"You're ferocious, little lady. Terrifying, even."

"Hand it over, Mister."

With a grin, he gave her the peace offering. Surprisingly, the drink was still hot, and every bit as strong as she liked.

"And you are correct." He waited until she'd had a second sip before speaking again. "I do have ulterior motives."

"Mmm-hmm." Over the rim of the cup, she regarded him. "I knew it."

He scooted closer to her, and every one of her synapses fired. "But first..." He brushed his lips across her forehead, then took away her beverage and kissed her mouth.

"Ohhh, yes..." The taste made her ravenous for more.

"That will have to do for now."

She scowled.

"Definitely ferocious when you don't get your way."

"You're learning, cowboy."

"Cowboy?" He lifted an eyebrow. "Rather than Commander Walker?"

"Seems fitting."

"I'm liking it. And don't think I don't want to tie you up and fuck you."

"We could start the day a little later."

His eyes darkened, and she wondered who she'd suddenly become. He brought out a naughty side of her personality she hadn't known existed.

"Except for the fact we have company, and while I enjoy your screams of delight, I'm not certain you want others overhearing them."

"Company?"

"Deborah—my housekeeper—is here with her daughter."

"I'm glad you told me. Does that also explain why you're dressed?"

"That, and the fact I wanted to get ready for our date."

"Our what?" Elissa searched his eyes for signs of teasing, but yet he'd told her he rarely joked.

"I thought you'd like to get out, take a ride out to the creek on the four-wheeler. Deborah brought us a picnic basket and filled it with food and all the other stuff she said we need to go with it. If you want, we can take a bottle of wine. We can head out around noon, assuming you want to go and your schedule permits?"

"You're serious?"

He nodded.

"You had me at wine." If she hurried, she could get in a couple of hours of work, even chat with her parents and Mary, the night manager at the pub, before leaving.

She put aside her cup and tossed back the covers.

"Oh, my lady, now we're definitely going to be late..." His eyes darkened as he moved toward her to capture one of her bare breasts.

Her nipple lengthened as he flicked a thumbnail across it, and an involuntary groan escaped from between her lips. "Jacob, please..."

"Is that a yes, continue? Or a please stop?"

Both. She wanted him to suck her nipple deep into his mouth, but she knew where that would lead. And he was definitely right about the way she'd scream when he had his wicked way with her. "Can we continue this later?"

"You can count on it." He lowered his hand, and she sighed, as much from relief as from frustration. "I'll meet you downstairs."

Once she was alone, she momentarily closed her eyes. This relationship with Jacob was unlike anything she'd ever experienced, and she needed to be careful with her emotions. Circumstances had thrown them together, and in a matter of time—hours? days? weeks?—she'd be back in her Denver apartment, working at the pub while building her business and finding rare, precious moments for her art.

No matter how much a part of her wanted this to continue, it wouldn't last. It would do no good to think about anything beyond the moment.

Resolved, she finished her tea, then hurried through her

shower before dressing and going downstairs to meet the housekeeper.

Deborah was a tall, beautiful woman with a quick, welcoming smile, and she wore a T-shirt that read GOING DOWNHILL FAST. "Morning! You must be Elissa."

"It's nice to meet you."

"Jacob's been telling me all about you."

"Has he?" She scowled at Jacob, who was leaning against the counter, a cup of coffee in hand.

With a grin, he shrugged.

"I hear you're quite an artist."

"Ah…" Elissa cleared her throat. Just what had he said? Surely he hadn't mentioned her erotic images.

"You're working on a corporate logo for a motivational speaker?"

She released a breath she hadn't realized she was holding.

"I'm writing a children's book."

"Are you?"

"The main character is going to be a ski bunny."

"Your T-shirt… Obviously a skiing reference?"

"Yeah. I'm an instructor."

"Deborah is being modest." Jacob drained his cup, then slid it onto the counter. "She used to compete for the women's alpine team."

With her mouth open, Elissa looked back at Deborah. "Seriously?"

She nodded. "Until I blew out a knee one too many times. Still love it, though."

"Your celebrity will be a huge advantage."

"That's kind of you to say, but I'm sure no one remembers who I am."

Elissa's creativity was sparked. "Do you have a website?"

"No. Should I have one?"

"Absolutely yes. Do you mind if I come up with a couple of ideas for you?"

"Are you kidding me right now? I mean, I can pay you a little bit, but—"

"Say no more. It's been a while since images have come to me this rapidly." And the Bonds computer would make working on them pure pleasure. "Do you have any concept drawings of your ski bunny?"

Deborah shook her head. "I don't have any talent in that area, and I haven't started looking for an illustrator yet."

"How about a color concept?"

"I was thinking along the lines of something like green or yellow."

Elissa nodded. "Bright? More muted?"

"Whatever inspires girls to go for their dreams."

"I love it."

At that moment, a young child walked in, clutching the massive, squirming Waffle against her chest.

"This is my inspiration." Deborah smiled. "My daughter, Adele."

Elissa grinned. Waffle's back was against the child's tummy, and the cat's large front paws hung over Adele's forearm.

"Honey, say hello, and put down the cat."

Rather than doing as her mother said, Adele held Waffle tighter. "But I love her, and she likes it."

Elissa was surprised Waffle tolerated being held at all.

Deborah sighed. "Do I need to repeat myself?" Though Deborah didn't raise her voice, her words were firm.

Chin set at a stubborn angle, Adele did as she was told. Shockingly, Waffle plopped her enormous body down at the girl's feet.

"And say hello to Miss Elissa," Deborah prompted again.

"Hi." She offered a tiny wave.

"Nice to meet you, Adele."

"There's a teacher in-service at the preschool today, so we're driving to Steamboat for a little shopping."

Adele grinned, evidently forgetting all about the cat. "And ice cream!"

"Of course. How could I forget?" Deborah glanced at Jacob. "Picnic basket is on the table, and remember to use the ice packs I put in the freezer. Is there anything else you need before we leave?"

"That should be it," he responded. "I appreciate your stopping by."

"I'll send you some ideas for your website—and maybe even the bunny—in the next couple of days," Elissa promised.

"I'm so excited. Thank you."

After exchanging contact information, they hugged goodbye. And then Adele ran over. "Me too!"

Elissa crouched. "Of course."

For a quick second, Adele wrapped her arms around Elissa's neck before hurrying away to chase Waffle into the living room.

"I guess we'll be going for real now." Deborah grinned.

Jacob said he was going to walk them to the car and promised to be right back.

When the door closed, the house was suddenly silent, and Elissa stood there, staring, a dozen different thoughts and feelings racing through her.

Her days were consumed with work, and it had been a long time since she'd dated or even thought about the future.

But seeing Deborah and Adele together had made her wonder what she was missing.

The love between the mother and daughter reminded Elissa of what she shared with her own mom. And would she ever feel that with her own child?

Fortunately Jacob returned, interrupting her musings.

"Deborah liked you."

"It's mutual." To keep herself busy, Elissa turned on the kettle. "How did she become your housekeeper?"

"She's the sister of one of my ranch hands. Left a bad relationship right before Adele was born, and we put her in one of the property's cabins while she got back on her feet. She refused to accept what she called charity, so she insisted on doing some work around here. At this point, I'm not sure how I'd manage without her."

"Adele is wonderful. And even Waffle seems to like her."

"That says something." He grinned. "She's smart for her age, too. And she shows an aptitude for skiing, like her mother." He placed his cup in the sink. "Can you be ready to leave around twelve?"

"That's perfect." Even if he wanted to head out in ten minutes, she'd make sure she was ready.

"I'll meet you back here then."

She nodded.

Once again she was aware of how big the house was, and for the first time in her life, a pang of loneliness assailed her.

The strange emotions had to be a result of the even stranger circumstances, she reached for the box of pastries sitting on the counter. Bypassing the apple fritter and several eclairs, she grabbed a chocolate-covered chocolate doughnut, complete with sprinkles.

After she'd devoured it and brushed off her hands, she finished brewing her tea, then carried it outside.

She paused for a second to take in the view from the patio, refusing to admit the truth to herself—that she was hoping to catch a glimpse of Jacob in the distance.

With the drink cooling, she continued toward the garage apartment. Waffle darted in front of her, nearly tripping her as she opened the door.

The cat wound her way between Elissa's legs before racing up the stairs. "I see you're joining me."

Inside, Waffle found a patch of sunshine and dropped down to groom herself.

Before starting work, Elissa made calls home to talk to her parents and to check in with the bar.

Once she'd powered up the computer and settled into her chair, her creative energy flowed. The previous day, she'd been stifled, but now, inspiration danced from her fingertips.

It took only a couple of minutes to decide on her final choices for the motivational speaker's color palette. It was a shade darker than she'd been working with, and the change made the logo pop.

Less than two hours later, she'd added a couple of finishing flourishes to the logo and drafted a mock-up of his website's landing page. Finally satisfied, she sent the files to her client for his approval.

Then, captivated by Deborah's excitement about the ski bunny, Elissa spent another hour sketching out a couple of versions of the cartoon bunny.

She was deep in concentration when a notification skittered across the bottom of her screen, signaling an email from her client. Curious to know if he was pleased, she clicked through to find he was more than happy. *"Yes!"* She fist-bumped the air, and Waffle shot her a narrowed-eye sleepy glare. "Oh. Sorry. Didn't mean to disturb Your Majesty." Elissa had never had pets, and she was enjoying the feline's companionship.

Elissa promised the vector file to her client within twenty-four hours and asked him to supply pictures and videos, along with text to populate the actual website. Elissa shut down the computer and headed back outside, Waffle trailing behind her.

A noise captured Elissa's attention, and she paused. Moments later, Jacob drove up in a red all-terrain vehicle.

Instead of continuing on inside, she waited for him, admiring the way sunlight glinted off his dark hair. Even across the distance, she was aware of his gaze, and shivered anew at the way she'd come undone for him.

When he reached her side, he shut off the loud, rumbling beast and climbed out of the bucket seat. "Your ride, ma'am."

"I'm impressed." The machine had half doors, and the front part had a cover over it. "I imagined it would be a little more rugged than that."

"In what way?"

"I thought I'd be sitting behind you."

"You're thinking of a quad—all-terrain vehicle. Generally carries one person. This is a UTV—a utility task vehicle. It hauls cargo and can pull a small trailer. The seats are actually comfortable. Has heat and air-conditioning. Even a sound system." He cocked his head to one side. "But the idea of you straddling me and holding on tight has me rethinking my decision."

The image made her squirm, just as he'd no doubt intended. "This one's fine. Great even." Her tone was somewhere between prim and squeaky, and she cleared her throat.

He grinned. "Of course, we can save that for this evening."

For a moment, her heart skittered. She'd hated the idea of coming to his ranch, and yet all of a sudden she didn't want to leave. Denver and the outside world seemed so far away.

"I'll grab the picnic basket if you want to get a couple of towels from the hall closet."

"Why do we need towels?"

"So you can dry off after you get out of the water." He grinned.

"You might remember I don't have a swimsuit."

"Yeah. That's right." His grin turned feral. "There's a

camping blanket in there too. Something for us to sit on. Or for me to ravish you on."

She shivered. His words excited her more than she could ever admit. "Oh no. No no no. *No.* Nuh-uh. There shall be no public ravishing, Cowboy."

His eyes narrowed. "Challenge accepted."

"That's not what I meant." Or was it? She cleared her throat. God. The way he looked at her... It might be impossible to deny him anything.

"You may want a hat. Or something to keep the hair out of your face."

She nodded, then hurried inside. While she was there, she changed into a pair of shorts, telling herself it wasn't because they'd be easier to get out of than her jeans were. As she'd already told him, she wasn't the type of woman who skinny-dipped or who made love outside—not ever.

Within minutes, carrying the items he'd requested, she rejoined him.

Very slowly, very thoroughly, very approvingly, he swept his gaze over her, lingering on her bare legs. "You're a beautiful woman, Elissa."

His words were laced with conviction. She'd never seen herself as anything other than ordinary, but she had no doubt he meant what he said, and for the first time in her life, she saw herself the way he did.

"You ready?"

"Yes. I'm excited."

He placed the picnic basket and a bottle of wine inside a storage box, then stacked the blanket and towels on top. After that, he added a folding table and a couple of collapsible chairs to the cargo area.

"I see we really don't need the blanket." Elissa propped one hand on her hip.

This time, there was no trace of a tease in his eyes.

Instead, his gaze was as dangerous as it was predatory. "Oh I assure you, we do."

Her pulse picked up a few extra beats. Silently she cursed her very feminine reaction to him. The more determined he was, the more she was attracted to him.

He helped her into the vehicle. "Buckle up, Elissa."

Was that a warning?

After donning a ball cap that had been on the floorboards, Jacob climbed in next to her. Then he grabbed his cell phone and activated a button on its side. "Wildflower on the move. And we'd like some privacy."

"Roger that."

Without another word, he slid the device into a plastic holder attached to the dash.

"For a minute, I actually forgot why I was here."

"Good. I want you to relax."

Even though she honestly believed there was no real threat, there were constant reminders.

"We're doing our best to keep the intrusions to a minimum." He started the vehicle and headed down a narrow dirt road, in the direction of the distant Saddle Mountain.

"So who were you talking to?"

"Lifeguard."

She waited for him to go on. Instead, he focused on the road in front of him, features inscrutable. "Are you going to tell me anything more?"

"He's a coordinator, of sorts."

"Is this part of you trying to keep the intrusions to a minimum?"

After sparing her a quick glance, he nodded. "It's a balancing act. There's a lot of activity in the background that you don't see. And you have a right to the information you want to receive."

She was more curious than ever. "You said the man on the phone is a coordinator, of sorts. What does that mean?"

"When we're running ops, he oversees them. No one knows more about the nitty-gritty details of how Hawkeye is organized than he does. He works out of a control center where he monitors everything and provides us with any assistance required."

As much as the safety belt would allow, she angled her body toward him. "Go on."

"He has our backs—handles any emergency call from anywhere on the planet and dispatches appropriate resources. Police. Fire. EMT. FBI." Jacob paused. He appeared to want to go on but didn't.

"And other people?"

He didn't respond. Instead, he deftly changed the conversation. "He was injured in combat, and he lost the use of his legs."

"Is he a friend of yours?"

He kept his gaze trained on the road ahead. "Yeah."

"And Hawkeye's?"

"We go way back."

"To the service? Peru?"

"Astute guess. When you go through something like that, it changes you. Those of us who made it out are still close. Well, except for one guy."

She remained quiet, studying him. A line furrowed between his eyebrows, and his lips were set. Lost in the past? "I'm sorry. I shouldn't pry."

"It was a long time ago."

"But you still never talk about it."

"No. I don't."

What must it be like to have seen so many horrors and to continue on? Jacob found solace in the land, while Hawkeye still sought refuge in his work. "And you don't forget." It was more of an insight than a question.

Just when she thought Jacob might ignore her, he reengaged in the conversation. "I moved on. That's the best I can hope for. Hawkeye is as loyal as they come, never forgets his men or their capabilities. He believes in people, even when they've lost faith in themselves. And Lifeguard? Taking care of us—protecting us—is his purpose. It drives him."

"What kind of phone is that?"

"Designed by—"

"Bonds?" It was a guess, but no doubt a good one.

"It has a few extra features that are useful in an emergency. He has one that allows him to see holograms."

"That—*what?* Like in the movies?"

"Entertaining as hell, but I'm not sure how useful it is. I generally like to keep my discussions more private."

"From what I've read, he's constantly dreaming up new ideas. Some of them are just for his amusement."

"Probably accurate."

A minute later, he stopped the UTV to point out a mule deer. As if realizing she was being watched, the animal froze, staring back with enormous eyes.

When they remained in the vehicle, she eventually looked away and began grazing again.

"Thank you. That was amazing."

"I thought you might like it."

A few minutes later, he hit a big bump, tossing her around, and she grinned. "This is fun."

"Fun? In that case, I'll let you drive us back."

"I'd like that." She took in the endless expanse of sky and a few puffy clouds. Because of their speed, the breeze managed to whip a few errant strands of hair across her cheeks.

Less than half an hour later, he braked to a stop in a small clearing.

After unbuckling, she joined him at the back of the vehicle. The ground was carpeted in green, and a few shrubs sprang from the earth. "This is a wonderful spot. So beautiful, peaceful."

"I couldn't agree more."

While he set up the table and chairs, she wandered down to the river. Because it was only a tributary, it wasn't wide, and it was shallower than she expected. Colorful river rocks adorned the bed, and water burbled along invitingly. She crouched to test the temperature, then pulled her hand back against the bite of the chill. "It's freezing!"

"When the sun heats you up, you won't be able to resist the temptation of getting naked," he called back.

"You *are* persistent."

"I haven't even started turning on the charm yet."

Shaking her head, she returned to the makeshift campsite. He'd covered the table with a red-and-white-checkered cloth, and the picnic basket sat on top.

"Are you ready to eat?"

"I can wait for a little while."

"Good. That's what I was hoping to hear."

She shivered. "Do you ever stop?"

"Tell me honestly..." He thumbed back the bill of his baseball cap. "Do you want me to?"

The world went silent for a moment, and she found the courage to admit her truth. "No."

"Then we're in agreement." Gently, he captured her chin.

Her heart fluttered like a butterfly's wings. Even though she'd known him only a short amount of time, she craved him.

The intensity of his kiss shocked her. Rather than relaxed, it was urgent, and she responded to his passion, meeting each thrust of his tongue with a parry of her own.

He made her heart hammer and her thoughts swoon.

When her knees buckled, he caught her and pulled her tight against his chest.

"I've got you, Elissa."

Recognizing the inevitable, she surrendered. *"Yes."*

Jacob captured her mouth a second time. He slid his palm against her buttocks, pressing her against his pelvis. His cock was already hard, and the knowledge he wanted her turned her on. Response flooded through her, and she wrapped her arms around his neck, silently giving more than he asked.

He released her momentarily, long enough to search her features and to thread his fingers into her ponytail. His grip firm, he held her in place as he sought her lips once again, devouring her moans and whimpered pleas.

Desperate for more, she wrapped her arms around his neck and lifted her heels so she could move her hips against his.

He needed no other hints. "I'm going to make love to you."

Shocked that she needed his possession more than her next breath, she nodded and reached for his belt.

Within seconds, he'd taken over, pulling her shirt off over her head and unhooking her bra, seemingly all in the same sweeping move.

In the breeze, her nipples instantly hardened.

"Nice." He bent his head to suck one into his mouth, and desire plowed through her.

"Tell me you have condoms." She had to ask before common sense fled entirely.

"Always. I consider that essential equipment now that you're around, fair Elissa."

Thank God.

He removed his shirt and draped it around her shoulders, then left her only long enough to spread out the blanket and grab his cell phone. Something else he obviously considered essential.

Then he opened the metal button at her waistband. Looking in her eyes, he lowered the zipper. Instead of pulling her shorts off, he slid his hand inside, then brushed aside the gusset of her panties to stroke her clit.

At his light touch, she moaned.

"You're already wet, aren't you?"

"Mmm." He coaxed responses from her that she didn't know she was capable of.

As he continued to work his magic, she clamped her hands on his biceps for support and allowed her eyes to drift closed.

"Come for me, Elissa. No holding back."

His rough command melded with his masterful touch, lighting a fire deep in her. Within seconds, whimpering and crying, she climaxed, giving him what he demanded, as if it could be any other way.

Finally, when her breathing returned to normal and the brain fog cleared, she looked at him.

Maybe it was a trick of the sunlight, but she read purposeful intent in his dark green eyes.

"I need to be inside you, Elissa."

She nodded. Rather than satiating her, the orgasm had only made her crave him more.

After he guided her to the blanket, he tossed aside his hat. She reclined onto her elbows to watch as he shrugged off his lightweight jacket to reveal a gun holster.

He's carrying?

She shook her head. Of course he was. How could she think otherwise?

He covered the handgun with a towel, then tugged his T-shirt up, revealing the honed planes of his stomach. A shiver of arousal chased through her as he finished tugging the material over his head.

"See something you like?"

Elissa blushed. "I'll be honest, I've never been so fascinated by a male body before."

Showing zero embarrassment beneath her steady gaze, he gave her a quick grin. "And I meet your approval?"

A shiver tracing through her, she met his eyes. "You know you do." And she ached to explore every part of him with her fingers as well as her mouth.

He toed off his work boots and socks, then unfastened his belt before removing his jeans. His tight gray boxer briefs showcased his enormous erection. "You're ready for me, aren't you? Tell me you are."

"I always want you."

Jacob removed his underwear before stripping off her remaining garments. Within seconds he'd taken total control. He was lying on his back, and he captured her wrists to guide her on top of him.

"Couldn't get over the image of you like this, sitting up, wide open."

Being in nature, naked, straddling him, should have made her shy. Instead, his approval emboldened her.

He toyed with her pussy to ensure she was lubricated, allowing her to set the pace.

Since her insides were a little tender, she took him in small, measured strokes.

When he was all the way inside, he groaned. "My God, woman." He cradled her breasts, then tweaked her nipples.

The sensation—tenderness and pain in one—caused her to pitch forward. As she'd known he would, he caught her, protectively cradling her against him.

Then he grabbed hold of her ankles and tucked her feet

inside his thighs, forcing her knees even farther apart, seating himself even deeper inside her.

"I…" She whimpered.

"You can." After taking hold of her chin, he kissed her deeply and for so long that her senses were overwhelmed, and she no longer noticed the discomfort of him filling her. "Touch yourself for me."

With as tight as he was holding her, it took some maneuvering for her to slide a finger across her swollen clit.

"That's it, Elissa."

He grasped her waist, steadying her as his powerful hips pistoned and he fucked her hard, seemingly with no restraint —not that she would deny him anything.

She was rising and falling on him, finding her climax when he moaned. How incredible this was, knowing he was on the verge.

Elissa lifted her head enough to watch him in fascination, adoring the way his lips pressed together and his jaw tightened.

His breaths were shallow, and he bit out her name, along with a soft curse.

The forceful way he came in her sent her over the edge, but he was there for her, clasping her again, murmuring reassuring words in her ear.

It wasn't until long minutes later that she became aware of the sounds around her—the burbling water, the cry of a hawk. She managed to slow her breathing and regain her bearings long enough to press a palm against his chest in order to sit up. She blinked against the sunlight and saw his triumphant smile.

"I think you liked that."

"More than a little." The admission was easier than she imagined it might be.

"Then I think you'll also enjoy my next suggestion." Using

his superior strength, he managed to roll them over, leaving her pinned helplessly beneath him.

"Oh?" Skeptically, she raised her eyebrows.

"Skinny-dipping."

"I… Uh." She drew a breath. "We've had that discussion before. I don't do that kind of thing."

"Until five minutes ago, you didn't have sex outside either."

"But…"

"You have to admit, it will feel nice after being hot and sweaty."

No doubt he was right about that. Because there were no clouds, her skin was warm.

Unabashed, he stood and crossed to the four-wheeler. She sat up and watched as he discarded the condom, then grabbed two towels. He tossed one to her. "You can preserve your modesty with this."

"It's a little late for that."

"That's not a bad thing." He strode to the water and stepped in. "Cold, but not frigid." He crouched to pour a handful of the pure Rocky Mountain water over his chest and half-hard cock. "You'll love it."

"I don't know about that." Despite her reservations, she was tempted.

"Have I led you astray?"

"Not *yet*."

As if conceding her point, he grinned. "Never know when you will get another chance." He extended a hand toward her. "Live a little. Promise I'll keep you warm."

CHAPTER SEVEN

HAWKEYE

Clutching the towel closed, Elissa walked to the water's edge.

"So very brave."

She still wasn't convinced.

"It's okay once you get used to it." Eyes dancing with a wicked gleam, he scooped up a handful of water and flicked it in her direction.

That was the motivation she needed.

After dropping the towel, she waded in, gritting her teeth against the temperature shock. "Look, Mister..." She crouched to return the favor, splashing him hard enough to drench him.

He took it like a man, standing there grinning even as droplets raced down his chest and thighs. "Do it again. Only this time come closer."

Was that a threat? Or an invitation?

Either way, she couldn't resist him.

After taking two tentative steps toward him, she bent over. His reactions were lightning fast. He swept her up and dragged her against him, holding her close, pressing one palm against her buttocks and the other between her shoulder blades.

"Your nipples are hard."

"You said you'd warm me up."

His eyes telegraphed his intent, and she obediently tipped her head back to accept his kiss.

He claimed her, plundered, then silently promised her more. And she wanted everything he offered.

By the time he pulled back, she was shaking from a fresh wave of desire. And even though she expected him to release her, his grip was firm.

"Admit it. I was right. It's better than you thought it would be."

Against her, his cock began to harden again.

"Yes." Everything was. *The sex. His kiss. Skinny-dipping.* "Much better."

He brushed his lips across her forehead before letting her go.

Now that they weren't playing, the chill crept back in. She made her way to the river's edge to pick up her towel and wrap it around her before finding a large, warm rock to sit on.

"I think we have a bottle of chardonnay in the picnic basket. Shall I pour you a glass?"

"Please." She should help, but she was so comfortable that she didn't want to leave her spot.

A few minutes later, he joined her. He'd pulled on a pair of shorts but hadn't bothered to dry off. Was he immune to the cold, as well as everything else that bothered mere mortals?

"Scoot over."

She wiggled over a few inches, enough to give him a little room. Then she accepted the plastic tumbler he offered her.

After sitting next to her, he tipped his glass toward hers. "Not a bad way to spend an afternoon."

They clinked their rims together.

"Actually I can't think of anything better."

He raised an eyebrow. "Still feeling like a prisoner?"

There were reminders, constant ones. But they'd faded into the background. "Not as much. I really needed this."

"Good. I have other ideas on how to keep you occupied."

So did she.

"Food."

She blinked. *"Food?"*

"What did you think I was talking about?" Jacob's voice held a light tease.

Right now, he was so different from the serious cowboy who'd kidnapped her and the implacable Dom who'd tied her up and sent shockwaves of orgasms through her body.

She liked every side of him and marveled at how much more emotionally revealing he was than any other man she'd ever been with.

"I'll set out the picnic, and you can join me when you're ready."

Once she'd finished her wine, she shimmied back into her clothes. No way would she ever be as comfortable with near nudity as he was.

Deborah had provided everything they might need, including utensils, plates, and napkins. The feast included fresh guacamole and tortilla chips, sandwiches on thick, crusty bread, olives, and a brick of cheese with apple slices as an accompaniment. There was also a delicious-looking assortment of cookies and brownies—not that Elissa needed them after this morning's doughnut. "This looks amazing."

After filling their plates, they sat in the chairs to enjoy the meal.

"Are you really going to come up with an idea for Deborah's ski bunny? Or were you being polite?"

"I already have. But if she wants me to illustrate the children's book? I'll need a pseudonym."

"Because of the work you're doing on the portrait for me?"

"I never said I'd complete it."

"Then why else would you need a pseudonym?" With a triumphant grin, he stood, then offered to take her empty plate.

He'd won. And they both knew it.

An hour or so later, he dressed and loaded up the UTV. "Still want to drive it?"

"Really? You meant it?"

Once she was behind the wheel, he gave her a few quick instructions.

She accelerated and was shocked by the responsiveness. Quickly she backed off the throttle, then looked in his direction with her mouth parted from shock.

"Top speed is about sixty miles an hour."

That seemed really fast for this machine. "Am I scaring you?"

"It would take a whole lot more than that, Elissa."

She set a comfortable pace while he updated Lifeguard on their status.

While she drove, he scrolled through his phone before finally sliding it back into the compartment on the dash. "How many kids do you want?"

"Me?" Elissa took her eyes off the makeshift road long enough to glance at him again "Why are you asking?"

"You asked me."

"But that was related to the ranch. Passing the land to the next generation."

"You're working with Deborah, and Adele really liked

you." He adjusted his ball cap. "Seemed like a logical extension to me."

"I've been so busy with life that I hadn't given a lot of consideration to being a mom." And this discussion would be easier if she wasn't sitting so close to a man she could suddenly picture as the father of her children.

"Hypothetically, then. Would you like to have kids?"

She flexed her fingers on the steering wheel. "I guess so. Yes."

"How many?"

For a moment, she considered her answer. "Two? Maybe three."

"I was thinking the same thing."

The summer air was suddenly too hot to breathe. *"What?"*

"I gave your question some more thought. Four sounds like a good number. Close in age. What do you think?"

They were having two separate conversations, weren't they? He couldn't possibly be talking about—thinking about—having babies with her. "Four?" The pitch of her voice was high and squeaky.

"Hypothetical children. Four's a good number, don't you agree?"

Heat, warm and liquid, flowed through her at the idea of having his children.

"This is hypothetical, right?"

"Until it's not."

He reached over to steady the steering wheel, and that's when she realized she was dangerously skirting the edge of the road.

"We can start with two and figure it out from there."

"Jacob..."

His phone rang. Without apology, he answered it. For minutes, while she sat there, thoughts swirling, he discussed ranch business.

As she braked to a stop near the house, he ended the call, with a promise to get back to the person he was talking to.

She exited the vehicle, and he joined her at the front of it. "I've got some work to do. Sorry. How about I join you for dinner in an hour or two? I'll cook."

A little time alone suited her fine.

Jacob paused for a second to trace her jawbone before striding into the house. She opted for a quick shower after being outdoors all afternoon...and having sex with him in the wide open.

When she returned to the main level, there was no sign of Jacob, and she was restless. After pouring a glass of wine, she headed back to her office, Waffle darting ahead, constantly underfoot.

Pulled by creative energy, she opened the image she was creating for him. Who was she trying to fool? From the moment he'd asked for it, it belonged to him, much like she did.

Chardonnay pushed to the side, she went back to work, darkening the submissive's hair and changing her eyes to blue.

She realized what had been confounding her—it was the muted emotion in the picture. While there was some, she wanted people who saw it to gasp at the realness of what was happening between the Dominant and his submissive.

But after surrendering to Jacob last night, and what they'd shared today, she was different. More open. More vulnerable. Maybe a little apprehensive. And she intended to infuse the image with the depth of her feelings.

Determined, she began her edits, dramatically changing the scene. She moved the woman's hair aside to expose her face. Then she altered the tilt of her chin. And now, instead of having her gaze cast down, the submissive looked up at her Dom through a fringe of lashes. Adoration melded with trust to create… Love.

Time stood still as she made hundreds of tiny corrections to the draft. Then, once she was satisfied, she pushed back from the desk and exhaled.

"Jesus." Jacob's single whispered word was heartfelt, and she knew the changes she'd made were the right ones.

She hadn't consciously heard him enter the apartment, but she'd known he was there. Every part of her recognized his presence and responded to it. She'd drawn inspiration from his comforting, commanding presence, even though he hadn't said a word.

Slowly she spun her chair to face him. He stood near the bar area, arms folded. His eyes were dark, radiating his approval.

"May I?"

"It's not the image you asked for. So if you'd like me to work on the other, I can. I still have the original saved."

As he crossed the room, she turned back to the monitor.

He stood behind her, hands tight on her shoulders. "It's even better than the previous version."

"I'm glad you're pleased." Now all she needed to do was translate it onto canvas, which would be a painstaking process—and worth every minute.

"But I want to see that expression in your eyes this evening."

She tipped her head back to meet his gaze.

"After dinner, I want you to present yourself to me in the dungeon. You'll wear my collar. This time, you'll ask me to put it on you."

His voice was confident, as if he didn't question her compliance.

"Be mine, Elissa."

That word again—*mine.*

Every time he said it, it became truer for her.

FOR THE FIFTH TIME IN AS MANY MINUTES, JACOB took his gaze off the camera feed in front of him and checked his watch. Eight o'clock couldn't come soon enough.

Earlier, they'd eaten dinner together, but Elissa had mostly pushed food around her plate. She'd been jumpy, as if nervous about their upcoming evening together.

Rather than soothing her, he'd slipped into Dom mode, telling her what time to meet him, and asking her to wear nothing other than his T-shirt when she arrived. Though he preferred her naked, until she was more comfortable, that was too big of a request.

After sending her upstairs to get ready for their evening ahead, he'd taken a shower, then headed to his command center to call Hawkeye. Of course the man hadn't answered, and now Jacob was reviewing tape from the day and glancing through the notes provided by the security team.

Nothing out of the ordinary. John Mansfield, the agent occupying the temporary guard shack near the ranch's gated entrance, reported the arrival of a delivery van at one thirty-seven p.m. The driver proceeded to the house and dropped off several boxes that Jacob had ordered. The van was logged back off the property fourteen minutes later.

All perimeter reports filed by Laurents and Johnson were clear.

The phone trilled with Hawkeye's ringtone. "Walker."

As expected, Hawkeye skipped ordinary pleasantries. "How's Wildflower?"

Though he knew his friend was hoping for a detailed answer, Jacob had no intention of revealing anything that wasn't necessary. "Adapting."

"That sounds promising."

Before Hawkeye dug for more information, Jacob seized control of the conversation. "What have you found out?"

"Not fucking enough."

The response was more honest than Jacob had expected.

"The list of my enemies is long."

"Narrowed it down?"

"According to the profilers we've got working on it, we're most likely looking for a man, though a woman can't be ruled out."

"Because of the anthrax."

"And the UNSUB is targeting people I care about."

Jacob nodded. In general, certain patterns of behavior were perpetrated by men. But women were known to use poisons. So the unknown subject could be either sex.

"We're looking at protective services cases where one of our clients got hurt or lost someone close to them."

"Or something from our ops overseas." Over the years, there'd been plenty of casualties, intentional as well as unfortunate, unintentional ones. "And there was a training accident at the compound."

"As I said, the list is long." Hawkeye's voice held a weary note. "We're assigning investigators to the targets that seem most likely."

It had to be asked. "Including Colombia?"

"Yeah."

Maybe if they'd been called in earlier, the Hawkeye team could have provided more help and had a better outcome. As it was, Melvin Rollins thought he could pay the hefty ransom and secure his daughter's release. Thirty-six hours after the money drop, there had been no sign of her. Frantic, Rollins had hired Hawkeye. But by the time Jacob and the rest of the team located her, she'd been dead—for less than two hours.

The abject horror and disappointment had killed his desire for any further involvement with security.

On the day of his daughter's funeral, Rollins had given a grief-stricken press conference, unfairly blaming Hawkeye Security for failing to mobilize faster.

"Rollins is supposedly out of the country at the moment."

Which didn't mean he was innocent, but it made him less likely a suspect.

"We're working twenty-four seven."

Which meant they were consuming a lot of resources.

"Keep Wildflower safe."

The idea of anyone harming her sent raw anger and fury surging in him. *They'd have to go through me first.*

He ended the call, then left his command center. In the hallway, he paused. Water was running, and the soft scent of lavender filled the air. That was all it took for him to be ravenous, his whole body demanding he possess her.

To steady himself, he dragged a hand through his hair.

He'd never been in love before, never understood why men did stupid things—wrote poetry, sent flowers, bought stupidly expensive rings, forgot common sense—when it came to women.

And now. Now he knew.

Because he was in danger of thinking about nothing other than her and the future he wanted them to create together.

Earlier, they'd talked about children. Until now, it had been little more than an abstract idea. His grandparents had wanted him to keep the ranch in the family, passing it on to their heirs. This afternoon, though, the idea took hold, and he couldn't shake it. He imagined spilling his hot seed inside Elissa's slick pussy, then seeing her pregnant with his baby.

He pictured their kids learning to ride horses, playing in the river, ice skating on a pond, traversing every inch of the land, then, as they were older, heading out on snowmobiles to find the perfect Christmas tree.

For a man who'd lived only for the present, this was a hell of a departure for him.

The house fell silent, and then the sound of a soft splash reached him.

Since less than an hour remained before she would join him, he jogged down the stairs. Unnecessarily he double-checked that all locks were engaged, and he informed the team they were in for the night.

Then he entered the dungeon to prepare it for her arrival.

He adjusted the room temperature so it was a little on the warm side. Since he intended to have her bare before him, he wanted her to be comfortable. He placed a couple of bottles of water in the refrigerator to chill, and he draped a lightweight blanket over the back of the chair. Even though it was summer, she might want to snuggle for comfort after the scene.

He checked the equipment he intended to use, making certain everything was in working order. Finally he completed two circuits around the space and stopped with his back to the fireplace, waiting.

Right on time, she arrived, pausing in the open doorway.

Her perfection took his breath away.

His T-shirt reached the middle of her thighs, and her hair brushed her shoulders. She looked at him with a mixture of trust and apprehension.

"I've been waiting for you."

Yesterday, their scene had progressed naturally, starting with a kiss. Tonight, he wanted to create something a little more formal, hoping to nudge her into a submissive headspace before they began. If his plan worked, tonight's experience would be even more pleasurable. "I'd like you to undress before entering."

Though she hesitated, she didn't protest.

In a single move, she pulled the material off and allowed it to fall to the floor.

Her nipples blossomed into tight buds, and she clasped her hands in front of her for a brief second before evidently realizing what she'd done. With a deep inhalation, she lowered her arms to her sides.

"Come to me, Elissa."

Nodding, she crossed to him, her bare feet silent on the floor. He'd decided against music. He wanted to hear her breaths, every sigh, moan, whimper.

"Uhm…"

"Kneel, my fair Elissa."

Her motions were perfect, artistry mixed with grace. "Open yourself. Your hands behind your neck with your shoulders and elbows turned back."

Once she did, he uttered words of praise. "Perfection. It's as if you're offering your breasts to me."

"Yes…Sir."

Generally when they spoke, her voice was strong. But here, there was a quiet submissive respect that he adored. She was still the confident woman he had fallen for, but she was willing to reveal a side she hid from the world. That was heady indeed, and he vowed to honor that trust. "Now spread your knees as far apart as you can."

Because she couldn't use her hands for balance, she made a couple of adjustments before settling in.

"Exactly as I like. This is what I mean when I ask you to open yourself."

"I'll remember."

He left her long enough to fetch a thin collar and a delicate leash. While the pieces weren't an exact match for the ones in the image she was working on for him, they were close enough. "Ask me."

Her voice wavered, barely above a whisper. "Please put your collar on me, Sir." Mouth slightly parted, she stared up at him while he fastened it in place.

He could repeat this act every day for the rest of his life and never tire of it.

Her breath caught when he attached the leash.

Holding the end, he took a step back, instantly recognizing that her picture had captured this moment in advance.

Her wildflower-blue eyes were wide with adoration. Though she'd never professed her love, he saw it in her gaze.

And he had no doubt the same was reflected in his.

More than ever, he was anxious for her to get on with the painting so he could have the portrait here where it belonged. "I'd like you on the top of the spanking bench."

"Of course, Sir."

Jacob offered no assistance while she stood, preferring to watch her sensual movements. "Go ahead. I'll follow you."

He remained where he was until the leash tightened, and she froze to look back at him.

Having her at his mercy like this made his cock hot and heavy, throbbing with need. "A perversion," he offered by way of apology. "I wanted to see what you would do." With enough force, the leash would snap. His control over her was not much more than an illusion, and without her permission, he held no power.

"And?" She tipped her head quizzically. "Is this a game? If so—"

"No." He held up a hand. "I promise you, it's not. We're simply exploring this part of our relationship. Continue."

This time, he followed her, close enough that the lead remained loose.

When she arrived at the bench, she placed a knee onto one of the siderails.

"I want you on your back, not your belly."

She looked over her shoulder. "Sir?"

"I have a few things in mind before I begin to torture you."

Her gulp of fear thrilled him. "Up you go. Then scoot to the end and part your thighs."

Once she was in place, he removed her leash and fastened it to one of his belt loops, then stood at the far end of the bench.

"I'm confused."

"I think what you mean is that you're being patient while awaiting your Dominant's next instruction."

"Yes. That's exactly what I meant. Sir."

Perfectly trusting. Perfectly compliant. Perfectly his. "There's a mirror on the wall to your right. Look at yourself."

Though she turned her head, it was his gaze she sought.

"Watch us."

As if to ask a question, she opened her mouth. A scant second later, she closed it again.

"Very good." He smiled, and in response she wriggled around a little before resettling. "Now, remembering my command to watch us, I want you to get yourself off."

She went rigid.

Rather than chastise her, he gently cupped her breasts, then squeezed them. In reaction, she moaned and arched her back.

Exerting a tiny bit more pressure, he leaned over to capture her mouth.

He took every bit of her sweetness and demanded more. When her tender mouth was swollen, he reluctantly ended the kiss.

While she watched, he pinched her sensitive nipples, and she gasped. "You're driving me mad."

"Good."

Without further prompting, she began to masturbate,

using her left hand to spread her labia while using her right index finger to stroke her clit.

Watching her get off while he played with her tits made his cock ache. Jacob had never been driven by lust, until she blazed into his life.

"Jacob... Sir..."

"Hold off a little longer."

She bit into her lower lip, and she moved her finger off her clit.

"I didn't give you permission to stop."

"But—"

"Or to argue. You may want to do as you're told before I change my mind about letting you have an orgasm at all."

In the mirror, her eyes pleaded with him. Delighting in the power of her obedience, he shook his head.

"It's pleasure." She whimpered. "And pain."

Jacob severed the connection of their gazes to look in the mirror attached to the wall in front of him. "You've allowed your thighs to close."

When she moaned instead of correcting her error, he tugged on her nipples harshly before releasing them.

"Oh! *Oh!* I'm going to come."

"My wonderful little sub enjoys a little nipple play? Good to know." His use of the mirrors provided an added dimension. She was compelled to stare at him, but he was looking at her pussy. She couldn't see him clearly enough to read his reactions. "But no orgasm yet."

"Ja-*cob!*"

"You may want to do as I said. Show me your clit. Let me see how swollen it is, how needy it is. And did I say you could stop playing with it?"

Elissa hiccupped a tiny cry. There was no artifice here, just pure feminine response to his dominance. Her abdominal muscles quivered as she parted her legs, then pulled back her pussy lips.

"Move your right hand to your tummy and keep that pretty cunt on display."

Her clit was as swollen as he'd hoped. That she'd held off her orgasm as long as she had was probably nothing short of a miracle.

Like a wolf, though, he was hungry for more. "It doesn't look at all like you need to climax."

"What?"

"You may continue."

She tore her gaze away from the mirror to look up at him. "Question, sub?"

Color fled from her face, as if she realized what she'd done. "No! I mean, no, Sir."

Because she didn't immediately correct her mistake, he slowly walked around to the far end of the bench. "Perhaps you need a little assistance."

"I'm sorry, Jacob." Misery dripped from her words.

"Nothing to apologize for."

"Does this mean... Are you going to let me come?"

"If you were the Dominant, what would you do?"

"That's not a fair question."

"Is it not?" He slipped his forefinger inside her, then brushed her clit with the moisture. "Nevertheless, it's one I'd like an answer to."

She curled her right hand into a tight fist.

"Waiting." Enjoying her ever-more frantic movements, he flattened the pad of his finger on her clit.

"Fuck. Fuck, fuck, *fuck.*"

"Elissa? If you were me, what would you do to a submissive who can't control herself?"

"I guess..." She jerked her pelvis toward him, silently

begging him to get her off. "I'd make her come multiple times."

"Forced orgasms until she couldn't stand up or think?" *Wily.* He fought to suppress his grin. "You wouldn't deny her entirely and keep her on the edge?"

"No." She panted. "Absolutely not."

"So you'd do this…" He inserted two fingers inside her.

"Yes. Yes. That's it."

"And this?" He eased out, then slid forward again with three digits, stretching her. "Are you watching in the mirror?"

At his prompting, she turned her head to do as he said.

"I want you to see my fingers in your pussy."

Her muscles began to clamp down on him. Helplessly she struggled to press herself against his hand as she sought relief. "Please, Sir. Please?"

"You beg so pretty." He moved, then teased the entrance to her tightest hole with one of his pussy-slickened fingers. "You're getting so close to being rewarded."

"Oh God. I can't, Jacob." She jerked her hips in desperation. "I mean it. This is too much. Too, too much."

"You can. You can do this for me."

Tiny beads of sweat glistened on her chest. Had he ever pushed a submissive this far? And how much more could she —would she—take? Fuck, she was hot. Beyond amazing.

"I'm going to come."

"Of course." In the mirror, he captured her gaze. "In about a minute. Maybe two."

She squeezed her eyes shut. This time, he let her get lost in her head. "Count, breathe, anything to distract yourself from what I'm going to do next." Her body convulsed as he slowly finished inserting his finger into her ass.

Elissa cried his name over and over. The sound echoed

around the room, bringing him pure Dominant satisfaction. "Keep your labia spread, Elissa."

Her mouth parted, the only acknowledgment of his demand.

Still finger-fucking both of her holes, he bent to eat her pussy.

He filled her, consumed her.

Then she screamed as her entire body went rigid and her juices drenched his hand.

Before opening her eyes, she drank in long gulps of air. He eased his fingers out of her and helped her to move back a little on the bench so she could prop her feet on the siderail for support.

"You're even more beautiful when you come, Elissa."

She struggled to sit up, and he offered his forearm for leverage.

"That was…" With a sigh, she wrapped her arms around her. "I'm actually no longer sure what day it is."

"Then my job here is done."

Her eyes widened. "Really?"

He laughed. "Fear not. We haven't gotten started yet." A fact his cock was insistently reminding him of.

"That's a little frightening."

"Then, fair Elissa, you should be terrified." He left her long enough to wash his hands and grab her a bottle of water.

Since she was still a little shaky, he uncapped it for her before asking, "How much of a break do you need?"

After taking a sip, she offered the water back to him. "What do you have in mind, Sir?"

Pride in her surged through him. A sub who could keep up with his pace was priceless. "There's the small detail of your failure to keep your gaze on us while I was being generous enough to give you an orgasm."

Her breaths were shallow. "But wait." She glanced up at him, with hunger in her expression. "I can explain."

"Unnecessary."

"I'm throwing myself on your mercy, and your understanding nature."

He scoffed.

She blinked several times in quick succession.

"Did you just bat your eyelashes at me, submissive? Trying to manipulate me into going easier on you?"

"Me?" She pressed a hand to her heart in mock surprise. "I'd never do such a thing. Perhaps Sir is mistaken."

"Mmm. Not convinced, Elissa."

She shivered, more from anticipation than fear, he surmised. "Let's attach you to the bench in a more conventional way, shall we?"

He relished the sight of her as she straddled the top, then settled in. After she was in place, he grabbed some ties to hold her securely. "What's the appropriate punishment?"

"Forced orgasms, Sir."

Jacob laughed. Her response had been too quick, as if she'd prepared in advance. "Try again."

"Uhm..." She moved around until she could see him. "A spanking?"

"And you'll watch from beginning to end?"

"I'll keep my eyes open this time, Sir."

If she became as lost in pleasure as he intended, there would be no way for her to do as she promised. He strode across the room to select a small leather flogger.

When he returned to the bench, her body was supple with relaxation, despite her bonds. In fact, they seemed to free her. "Gorgeous."

"Touch me?"

As if he could refuse her anything. Gently he rubbed her back and shoulders.

Her breaths became deeper, and she sighed. "Could we do this all night?"

"We could. Maybe a little oil and candlelight?"

"Sounds nice. But I'd prefer something a little different."

Their gazes met in the mirror, and she gave him a soft, serene smile he would never forget.

"I can get a massage at any spa. But I've never had another experience like this. I'd rather scene with you."

With long, slow motions, Jacob moved lower until he reached her buttocks. Then he increased the pressure to warm her up.

He continued, until even the backs of her thighs were light pink color.

Only when he was sure she was ready did he pick up the flogger.

For the first few minutes, she was able to keep her vow. Then as he heightened the intensity, she rested her cheek on the vinyl pad and seemed to fall into a light sleep. "Are you with me, Elissa?"

"Mmm-hmm."

He was flogging her in earnest now, leaving small welts on her skin. The more intense his strokes, the more approving her feminine little sounds.

Slowly he eased off, bringing her back to reality.

"Elissa?" He brushed strands of hair back so he could read her expression.

"Will you fuck me, Sir?"

Consumed by desire, he released her from bondage. "Please situate yourself at the end of the bench."

"Yes, Sir."

While she got into position, he undressed and rolled a condom down his cock. One day, in the not-too distant future, they'd be making babies instead of worrying about contraception.

Her buttocks were still hot from his spanking, making him groan. This woman would be his undoing.

"I need you in me."

Instead of taking her as he wanted, he fingered her clit, just to be sure she was ready. The little bundle of nerves hardened, and she moaned, arching her back as she offered herself to him.

The scent of her arousal was an aphrodisiac, and his need could no longer be contained.

Jacob eased his cock into her and began to stroke.

"This..." She tightened her buttocks as she rocked back and forth. "Yes..."

"Elissa..." He dug his fingertips into her hipbones and dragged her back, allowing him even deeper inside her.

"Oh Jacob! Sir!"

"Press your breasts against the bench, then come for me."

He forced himself to hold back while she ground out a screaming climax. Over and over, she called his name. Her sounds and their friction were potent and primal, and he went rigid, gritting his teeth as he orgasmed in a long, hot stream.

She was breathing heavy, and she didn't move even as he withdrew.

"Stay where you are."

"Don't worry, Sir. I don't think I can stand up on my own."

He grinned, her comment making him stupidly happy.

After throwing away the condom, he crossed back to her, picking up the blanket on the way.

He wrapped it around her before helping her down.

When her feet were on the floor, her knees wobbled, so he scooped her up and carried her toward the chair in front of the fireplace.

"You sweeping me off my feet seems to be a bit of a habit."

"Objections?"

She pressed a hand to his chest. "Not even one."

"I kind of like it myself." He managed to sit while still holding her.

"So strong."

"Flattery, Elissa?"

"An observation, Sir."

Maybe. Regardless, her approval mattered, feeding the hungry wolf inside him. His woman was proud of him.

She snuggled against him, and he inhaled the subtle scent of her shampoo.

"When I have fantasies about BDSM, they're like this."

"In what way?"

"The aftercare. Well, and during care, too. I felt safe, which allowed me to completely let go. You don't seem impatient to get rid of me and get back to your real life."

Maybe he'd be able to make her understand that she *was* his real life.

"Honestly I've never had a scene like this before. Like you're genuinely concerned about me enjoying it, and you're not just going through the motions."

He'd likely been guilty of that when he was younger, and he cursed the insensitive bastard he'd been. Now his focus was Elissa, and her enjoyment was paramount.

"There's something different about being in a relationship with—" She broke off before sitting up and attempting to escape. "Not that we do. I mean, we're not, and you're not—"

"Stop." He tightened his arms around her waist, keeping her close, determined to nurture her emotions with the same ferocity that he'd protect her physical body. "We do have a relationship. When this is over, we'll figure it out. But I'm not prepared for you to walk out of my life without a backward glance." If necessary, he'd follow her to the ends of the earth.

"Jacob…" She placed a hand on her throat.

"How does your ass feel?"

As he'd hoped, her eyes darkened.

"Are you trying to distract me?"

"No more so than you were with me earlier." He grinned. "Answer my question, subbie."

"Fine. I guess." She wrinkled her nose. "What do you have in mind?"

His cock stirred.

"Oh." She bounced a little, making him even harder.

With her in his arms, he stood and carried her to his bedroom. "We've got a long night ahead of us, Elissa."

"Let's get started, Sir."

CHAPTER EIGHT

HAWKEYE

Consciousness teased the edges of her sleep, but Elissa didn't want to wake up. Instead, she pulled the comforter tighter around her and tried to drift off again. But clattering sounds continued to disturb her. And then there was the scent. Coffee. Even though it wasn't her preference, there was no denying its enticement.

Not inclined to give up, she opened her eyes long enough to find a pillow; then she pulled it over her head. As had been a habit since she'd arrived a week ago, she was in Jacob's bed. Protected in the comfort of his arms, she slept better than she ever had before. And waking up and having leisurely sex in the middle of the night was amazing.

He didn't need as much rest as she did, and most mornings he let her stay in bed as long as she wanted.

Even though she'd protested mightily at being kidnapped, the experience had been amazing.

Her creative energy had been higher than ever. She'd met the deadline for her client, and she'd started painting the piece Jacob had commissioned. Additionally she'd kept in contact with her parents at the pub. Joseph was still helping out, and they seemed happy, if a little tired.

Not only that, but her evenings were spent with Jacob, watching television, talking in front of the outdoor fire, or scening. Still, she couldn't get enough of him.

Without knocking, he entered the bedroom. "I brought you tea."

His bribe was almost enough to tempt her to remove the pillow. *Almost.* But after the intensity of last night's sex, she wanted rest more than anything.

"It's your favorite."

"Hmm."

"Earl Matcha, or somebody like that. Not sure who he is."

He was impossible, and every day he came up with innovative names for her drink. With a laugh, she tossed aside the pillow, then sat up and aimed it at him.

He ducked, avoiding contact, all without rattling the cup. "Stop with the missiles! I know the difference, honest. You drink Earl Grey in the morning because of the caffeine. Matcha is what you prefer in the afternoon. And it gets made in a whole different way. It's a lot more complicated and makes a green mess all over the counter."

For a moment, she lost her voice. Like that first morning, he was wearing nothing but shorts, and her reaction was visceral. Every time she saw him, he was even more breathtaking.

Already, they were building a history together, layers of memory, making him more complex. In addition to his stunning looks, he was infinitely gentle and patient with her. He cared for her during and after a scene and always, always made certain her needs were met.

How was she going to manage when this crisis was over and she was back at home, alone, and he was no longer part of her life? Though he'd reserved the right to talk about a future, one was impossible. His life was here, and hers was with her parents in Denver.

Trying to restore her equilibrium, she pretended everything was okay by saying the first thing that popped into her mind. "So what do I have to do to earn it?"

He looked at the drink, then back at her. "Well, considering it's the Earl with a splash of whole milk, I'd say the bar is pretty high."

"I have an idea."

"Do you, indeed?"

"Why don't you put the cup down, Sir?"

"As I've said before...anything for the lady." He placed it on the nightstand.

"Grab a condom while you're there." She'd never been the initiator before, and judging by the way he angled his head to one side, he liked her boldness. "Then bring your beautiful cock back to bed."

He grinned.

But not for long. Once he was lying on the bed, she stroked and licked him to hardness, sucking his length down her throat.

Digging his hands into her hair, he moaned. "Jesus, Elissa."

He began to pump harder. When she realized he was getting close to coming, she stopped what she was doing.

"You're a fucking goddess at that."

She couldn't help her triumphant grin.

"I had no idea you had that skill."

She didn't either. Until him, she had no interest in even trying. And she'd had no idea how thrilling it was to turn him on like that.

Somehow, even with her hand trembling, she managed to unwrap the condom, then sheathed him in it.

While he watched, she slid a finger inside herself, then

pulled it out to show him how much he aroused her. "You do this to me, Jacob."

"That's enough." He captured her hand to lick the glistening drop from her, then dragged her on top of him.

She leaned forward to brush a kiss against his mouth. His jaw was tight, showing his restraint.

Elissa adjusted her position, lifting herself up to guide his cockhead toward her pussy.

He was enormous, filling her completely, and she took a few breaths to relax while her body adjusted to the depth of his penetration. Because they had sex so often, her insides were still sore, but her need for his possession was too powerful to ask him to stop.

For the first couple of minutes, he allowed her to be in charge, and she rode him with slow, sexy, rhythmic undulations.

But then, inevitably, he growled. "You're fucking killing me, Elissa."

With that, he dug his fingers into her buttocks and lifted her higher with the next stroke, changing the pace, becoming more frenetic, hotter. Her breasts bounced, and her hair wildly swung back and forth. Every part of her was on fire from his possession.

She was lost in him.

Her orgasm loomed just beyond reach. As if knowing that, he moved one of his hands from her ass, licked a finger, then pressed it against her anal whorl. The pressure, combined with their motions, made her splinter. She came hard, and her body shattered beneath his relentless sensual assault.

Screaming, she pitched forward. As always, always, he caught her, wrapping her tight while she recovered. This time, however, he continued to rock his hips, sliding just the tip of his cock in and out.

The sensation was different, tingling, ratcheting her tension again.

Like the generous lover he was, Jacob brought her to a second climax before he unleashed his powerful control.

"Fuck. *Fuck.*" His body went rigid, and muscles and sinews contracted.

Watching him orgasm—seeing the result of their joining taking him apart—sent a rocket of feminine satisfaction arrowing down her spine.

They held on to each other until their breathing returned to normal, and she savored the moment.

Before she was ready—not that she ever really would be —he helped her to climb off him.

He rolled to his side and wrapped a lock of her hair around his hand. "That'll have to hold us."

"Can it be evening yet?"

"You, me, the dungeon at seven?"

"It's a date."

After pressing his thumbpad against her chin in a motion that was both affectionate and possessive, he climbed out of bed and headed for the bathroom. In the doorway, he stopped and looked back at her. "Oh, Elissa?"

"Hmm?"

"Your tea is cold."

"It was worth it." She grinned. "Most definitely worth it, Sir."

"Woot!" Elissa pushed Send on the email to her client, letting him know the final touches on his website were done, which meant the entire project was now complete. Online, the speaker's branding was consistent across all platforms, from social media to business card, making him appear professional as well as polished. She took a few minutes to finalize his invoice, which was almost as rewarding as finishing the actual work.

Right now, everything was perfect with the world—well, except for the fact that she could use a hot bath to ease the tension from her muscles, and it wasn't just from sitting in front of a computer for hours. It mostly had to do with the way Jacob had attached her to the Saint Andrew's cross and spent an hour having his wicked—and delicious—way with her last night—not that she was complaining.

The last two weeks with Jacob at his ranch had been amazing. Relaxing. Though she talked or video chatted with her parents at least once a day, the disconnect from her regular life had allowed her to see things differently and be more attuned to the wonders of nature around her.

Because of the mountain darkness, the number of stars at night was breathtaking. She'd downloaded an app so she could figure out which constellations and planets were visible, and she was starting to recognize them. A couple of times, she and Jacob had sat quietly near the firepit and watched the moonrise. She was enjoying it so much she was considering buying a telescope. Which she might actually do once her client paid his bill.

With a smile of satisfaction, she closed all of her client's files, then decided to take a quick break to celebrate and reset before working on Jacob's portrait.

That morning, he said he needed to work on some ranch business and provide guidance on some projects and help repair fence line. She'd walked him out to the UTV, and he'd promised to return midafternoon, and informed her that Hawkeye's agents were close.

One was stationed at the gate. Another was in proximity to the house. A third was patrolling the grounds a little farther out. They had a drone in the air, and it would patrol the grounds in segments. Jacob had a link to all the cameras on his cell phone. Radio checks would occur every thirty minutes, and Lifeguard was periodically monitoring the feeds.

Then, unmindful of anyone who might be watching, he'd given her a kiss so deep, coaxing a response so immediate and powerful that she had no doubt that he was the only man for her.

A peek out the window showed that Deborah was still at the main house, and Elissa looked forward to visiting with her for a few minutes. And a cup of matcha would be perfect to help her switch into a different frame of mind.

"Kettle's already turned on," Deborah said when Elissa slid open the patio door. "I saw you walking across."

"However much Jacob's paying you, you deserve a raise."

Deborah grinned. "I'll tell him you said so."

Outside, Waffle raised up on her haunches and pressed her front paws on the door. "She's a pest." Deborah sighed. "If she's inside, she wants to be out. If she's outside, she wants to be in."

"I can sort of relate," Elissa admitted. "Relaxing in the hot tub is always appealing when I'm cooped up in my office." Funny how she'd already claimed the garage apartment as hers. "But when I'm out there, I get all these ideas that make me want to be back at my computer."

Once she opened the door, the cat dashed in. In a blur, she ran past Elissa and jumped up on the counter to steal a piece of bacon.

"Shoo!" Deborah waved her arm, but Waffle was already running out of the room in a flurry of fur.

Elissa laughed. "She won that one."

"She has no manners at all. If she wasn't so darn lovable..." The kettle beeped, and steam escaped the spout.

Deborah used some of the boiling water to warm the inside of the ceramic teapot before starting to brew the matcha.

While waiting, Elissa perched on a barstool. "How's the book coming?"

"Slow. Every word is an effort, and I second-guess every one of them. Does it convey the right tone? Is it entertaining enough?" She sighed. "I always have three files open. The document, a dictionary, and a thesaurus. Every day I seem to remove more words than I add. I honestly had no idea how long this would take or how hard it would be to concentrate. Sometimes I think I'm my own worst enemy."

"Do you make up stories for Adele?"

Deborah nodded. "That's where the idea came from."

"Have you tried recording one and transcribing it? I mean, just doing it without judging it as you go?"

"As if." Deborah rolled her eyes, and Elissa laughed.

"How about a transcription service? You send the voice file, and they send you back text?"

"That's an interesting idea." Deborah leaned against the counter "When I'm at the computer, I think differently than when I'm just entertaining my kid, you know? And then I'm always second-guessing myself."

"It's an idea. I had a client who couldn't provide any of the verbiage he needed to complete his website, so he employed that technique. It hadn't been perfect, but at least they'd had something to edit." She shrugged.

"Might be worth a try."

"I've been playing with your website. Of course, I'd prefer everything to be in your voice, but I found some articles about you online, so I came up with a rough draft of your bio. I understand you're modest about your accomplishments, but that's the thing you'll need to stand out."

Deborah poured a cup of tea and slid it across the counter. "I'm not comfortable talking about myself."

"That's why I'm working on it for you." Elissa grinned. "And we need to start talking about social media, and you posting pictures from around the Steamboat area since you'll be using it for inspiration for your series of books."

Deborah gulped. "Series? I haven't finished one yet."

"Marketing. And you went right past me saying we need to get your social media in order."

She wagged a finger at Elissa. "That was tricky."

"Did you find an illustrator yet?"

"I'm still talking to a couple of artists."

"Let me know when you make a decision. I'll be happy to send over the files that you like."

"You know..." She picked up a dish towel and studied Elissa. "You've already done a lot of the work. I'm thinking about hiring you. I mean, you know my concept, and—"

"Wait." Elissa put down her cup. "Me? No. I can't."

"Now who's being modest?"

"You don't understand." She shook her head. "I love your ski bunny, but definitely don't think you want me working with you."

"You're talented."

"But..." How did she confess this? "I assume that Jacob hasn't told you what I'm painting for him?"

Deborah waited.

Would she have to get used to admitting this in the future? "Adult in nature."

"Oh?" The other woman blinked. *"Oh."*

"I'm honored that you'd think of me, but believe me when I tell you that I'm not the right person for a children's book."

"Could you use a different name? I mean, no one would have to know, right?"

Elissa and Jacob had jokingly tossed that idea around, but the truth was, she was happy with the direction her creativity was headed. "I'm happy to help you in any way, but..." She cleared her throat. "Anyway, I can always have a look at the project and give you some advice."

"So when do I get to see some of this other art of yours?"

"Are you serious?"

"Oh, shit yes. I spend so much time with my kiddo that I've forgotten what it's like to be a grown-up."

"In that case, I'll give you a peek when I have something I'm willing to share." This first one was so personal, an evolving reflection of what she shared with Jacob, that she wanted to keep it private.

"I can't wait." Deborah refilled Elissa's cup.

"Thanks."

"I always enjoy the break. It's nice having you here."

As far as Elissa knew, Deborah didn't know the whole story, and she hadn't asked.

"I'm going to finish up here since I need to pick up Adele from school."

"I'll let you get back to work. Give Adele a hug from me?"

"She can't wait to come see you again."

Maybe because they'd spent an hour coloring together at the kitchen table last week.

"And she misses Waffle too."

Now that Elissa had enjoyed a short break, she was reenergized.

"Tell Jacob I'll be back next week. Since Eric's on vacation, I brought over some groceries for you two. I also made a lasagna. It's in the fridge with some baking instructions. As you saw, I also fried some bacon—not that there are as many pieces as there were." She scowled at the cat, who didn't look up from bathing her paw after devouring her treat. "Anyway, I figured you could eat it with breakfast or make BLT sandwiches tomorrow. There are also a few meals in the freezer that Eric made, but if you need anything before I'm back, just give me a call. Other than avoiding my book, I don't have a lot going on this week."

Elissa laughed. "I've dealt with that with some of my design projects, so I totally understand." She slid off the barstool, then grabbed her cup.

"The pot's more than half full. Do you want to take it with you? There's a serving tray in the pantry."

"Good idea." Elissa located the lacquered piece, and once she had it loaded up, she said goodbye before opening the patio door. Waffle darted across the room, then dashed between Elissa's legs. She had to do a fancy sidestep to keep her balance.

"Be careful! That darn cat is going to end up tripping someone."

"She's definitely fast." And somehow managed to be everywhere at once.

When they were outside, Waffle raced toward one of the lounge chairs on the patio and jumped onto it. By the time Elissa reached the garage, the feline was already curled up and appeared to be sleeping.

Elissa topped off her tea and was about to wake up her computer when the sound of an approaching vehicle captured her attention.

Curious, she walked to the window that faced the house.

A large white panel van bearing the name of a well-known delivery company ambled up the driveway and parked.

The driver slowly exited, and she absently noted he wasn't carrying anything as he started up the path toward the porch. Then the vehicle's rear door exploded open, and another person—appearing to be a man, tall, dressed in black, with a ball cap pulled low to disguise his features—jumped out.

The delivery guy looked over his shoulder and hurried a little faster.

Sudden, hot fear slammed her heart into overdrive.

She told herself she was being ridiculous. All of Jacob and Hawkeye's fears had made her paranoid, and she was overreacting.

It was just a delivery.

But then the second man moved faster and appeared to stick something against the driver's spine and forced him up the steps.

Elissa jumped back, away from the window.

Think. She had to think.

Deborah was all alone in the house, and even if she didn't open the door, the men could get in through the patio. That would only take another minute or two.

And Jacob wasn't expected to return for another couple of hours. She wrapped her arms around her middle, silently assuring herself there were plenty of agents around. No doubt they were already aware of the situation and had it under control. In fact, maybe the man she'd seen was one of Hawkeye's men.

But what if he wasn't?

She remembered Jacob's admonishment to reach out to him for any reason. He'd rather it be a false alarm than to take any chances.

Hurriedly she rushed to the light switch and pushed the panic button.

She expected an alarm to ring—something, anything—but nothing happened. Was it even working?

Elissa returned to the window in time to see the door open. Then a shot rang out, the delivery driver crumpled, and the man dressed in black shoved his way into the house.

CHAPTER NINE

HAWKEYE

An alarm shrieked on Jacob's phone, splitting the silence. It wasn't an ordinary tone. It meant a panic button had been pushed somewhere. Cold fucking dread ripped through him.

He released the wire tightener he'd been using on the fencing and grabbed his phone from his belt clip to check the display. In neon green, the words GARAGE APARTMENT were flashing.

His training kicked in at the same time that anger flattened his heart rate.

Immediately he opened the video feed app even as he strode back toward the grouping of vehicles. He'd driven his utility vehicle, but one of the ranch hands had arrived on a tricked-out ATV that was significantly faster than his.

Though he didn't stop moving, he exhaled his relief when he saw Elissa staring out a window. He selected an option that would allow him to talk to her over the room's speaker system. "Elissa?"

"Jacob!" Her voice was wobbly. She looked around

instinctively, as if seeking him out. "He's in the house, and the delivery driver…" She gulped. "I…think he's dead."

He tried to understand what she meant, but he needed her safe while he did so. He took less than a second to brush the key on the side of his phone, alerting Lifeguard he was needed. "I need you to breathe. Stay calm. You've got information we need in order to end this situation. Do you understand?" He took a breath of his own and forced a note of calmness into his tone.

On the screen, he saw her nod.

"Is there anyone outside?"

"No. He's in the house, with Deborah."

Shoving away tendrils of panic, he focused himself on staying in the moment. This wasn't Peru or the attacked convoy in Colombia. He could and would get Elissa and Deborah through this safely. "Move away from the window and close the blinds, then walk over to the door and lock it."

There was no response, and she remained where she was, as if frozen to the spot.

"Elissa." He kept his words measured, reassuring but uncompromising. "Pay attention to the sound of my voice. Close the blinds." She was safer if no one knew she was in there. "Elissa?"

"Okay." She nodded as she pulled on the correct string.

"Good. Now I need you to lock the door. Do it for me. Do it *now*."

Finally she moved and threw the bolt home. He exhaled his relief. "Help's coming. I'm on the way." He signaled to the ranch hand who'd been riding the ATV. "Need your keys."

"Sure, boss."

Jacob caught them with one hand, then straddled the beast and fired it up before sliding the cell phone into a holder. Jacob gunned the throttle and raced toward the house.

Trying to stay in control of the four-wheeler, he pressed a key on the side of his cell phone that immediately connected him with Lifeguard. "Operation Wildflower. Got a situation at the ranch house. Need to know what I'm dealing with. Delivery person down? My housekeeper is inside with the UNSUB." Unknown subject. "And I'm on a fucking ATV."

"Roger that." As always, Lifeguard was unflappable.

"Get me a damn sitrep."

"Mansfield at the guard shack is down."

Goddamn fuck it to hell. Of course he was—he had to be. Deliveries were common enough, and Mansfield would have recognized the driver as someone who belonged on the premises, which left him vulnerable.

On the feed to the office apartment, he heard Elissa's soft, rapid breaths. "You're doing good, Elissa." To Lifeguard, he was abrupt. "Intel from the drone?"

"Redirecting. Johnson inbound from perimeter on ATV. No response from Laurents."

He prayed they were only dealing with one UNSUB.

"Jacob?"

Elissa's soft, frightened voice reached him, going straight to his soul. "I'm here, baby. I've got you." He would die before breaking his vow. "Stay with me. I need you to take a breath and tell me what you saw—in great detail. Don't leave out anything even if you think it's unimportant." He pressed the key to connect Lifeguard so he could overhear the details she was providing.

"A delivery van arrived, the same one that always comes, and the driver wasn't carrying any packages."

"Go on."

"There was a man behind him, and it looked as if he shoved something into the delivery guy's back. And I heard a shot. Oh God. Oh God. Oh God. He's inside, Jacob." Her voice caught on a sob.

He disconnected from Lifeguard. "Stay in the apartment unless I tell you otherwise. Promise me? I mean it."

After she agreed, he reopened the channel to Lifeguard. "You got eyes on the garage apartment?" Minutes seemed to drag on, while in reality, he knew no more than a few seconds had passed.

"She's clear. All around."

Jacob pushed out a ragged breath.

"We've got drone footage. Laurents is down. Could have been hit by the delivery van."

"Goddamn it."

"Unmoving male on the front porch. Replaying front door cam to see if we can get a hit on the person's image. House camera showing armed male in the kitchen. Woman tied to a chair. Crying. Appears to have red marks on her face."

Fucking fuck.

Jacob resisted barking orders. He'd seen Lifeguard in action. Even though he was relaying information in a measured tone, he was summing up the situation, entering information in a computer that would summon help, link in others, including Inamorata and Hawkeye. The entire strength of the organization was being harnessed.

Rationally, Jacob knew all that—the primal part of his brain had been activated. Nothing—nothing—was happening fast enough. Rather than following the road, he was making a straight line toward the ranch house, and there were still more than four miles to go. But in this moment, he was completely, terrifyingly useless to Deborah as well as the woman he loved.

"Johnson's inbound on an ATV. Was doing the outer perimeter check. ETA five minutes."

Adrenaline compelled Jacob to gun the engine even

harder, pushing the tricked-out machine to eighty miles per hour, despite the danger from the uneven terrain.

"Laurents here," a man broke in, breathing heavily. "On foot. Fucking delivery truck hit me. Vehicle's useless."

Thank God he was still alive.

Jacob switched back to the woman he loved, pretending a calm he didn't feel. "Still there, Elissa?"

"Yes."

"You're doing great."

Lifeguard broke in. "UNSUB is moving through the lower level of the house. Now upstairs, clearing the rooms."

Life was happening between a series of his heartbeats.

"UNSUB back downstairs. Moving through the living room."

Time was running out.

"UNSUB out the back patio door. Headed for the garage."

"Jacob? Someone is calling my name."

"Don't respond." He edged the ATV to eighty-five. "Fuck it to hell."

"At the garage door."

"Elissa, I'm going to keep silent so that no one hears us, okay? Help is less than two minutes away." He'd never been more helpless. "We'll keep you safe. Hang in there, baby."

"UNSUB in the garage."

At least the sonofabitch hadn't headed straight for the stairs, and that bought him a few more precious seconds.

"Back outside."

"I hear footsteps, Jacob."

"A minute, minute and a half, baby. I'm right here." Jacob focused on his destination, calculating his response. The assailant likely had no interest in killing Elissa. She was a better weapon against Hawkeye if she was alive. But harming her? That was a possibility. But not on his watch. Not ever fucking again. "When Johnson arrives, I want her to disable the van and my truck. I don't want him to be able to escape with Elissa."

"Roger that."

"Jacob!" Her whisper was frantic and breathless. "I don't know if I can do this."

"Sixty seconds, Elissa. Stay calm for one more minute. Don't say anything more. But I'll stay on the line. I'm here with you."

The ensuing silence was more awful than anything he could imagine.

"UNSUB outside the apartment door."

Knowing he was now close enough to be picked up on Lifeguard's video, Jacob clipped his phone back into place.

The moment he neared the garage, he cut the engine, jumping from the ATV before it completely stopped moving.

Fear sharpening his senses, he started to run.

An unholy shriek ripped through the air, followed by a crash and a thud.

Then a shot rang out, echoing in his ears.

Shouting her name, gun palmed, events unfolding in horrific slow motion, Jacob raced up the stairs.

When he arrived at the doorway, he took in the scene. The assailant was lying facedown on the floor, his gun in hand, aimed in Elissa's direction. Liquid oozed around him, and shards of pottery—some large, some small—were splintered like arrows.

She was huddled in the far corner, her knees upraised, clothing damp, staring straight ahead with blood dripping down one of her arms. His fury spiked. "You okay?"

She nodded, her body trembling.

Instead of going to her like instinct demanded, he focused on his training. He had to secure the scene.

He stepped over the hissing and spitting cat that was

somehow in the room and kicked the intruder's hand hard enough to break his grip on the gun. Uncaring whether or not he'd shattered bone, Jacob flipped the man over. *Christ.* "Rollins."

"Fuck off, Walker." Rollins lunged for Jacob's gun, and Jacob lashed out with his steel-toe boot, connecting with the man's jaw.

Jacob's effort was rewarded with a satisfying crunch.

And he wanted to do so much more. But his priorities were Elissa and Deborah. "You're lucky I don't fucking take you out."

"Like you murdered my little girl?"

He channeled his anger into a cold, calculating strike. "You killed her yourself, you motherfucker, with your swagger and your refusal to call in law enforcement. You waited until it was too late, then blamed everyone else. You deserve to go down. Sins of the father."

Rollins sneered. "Fuck you."

"You'll live with Shayley's death for the rest of your life. And you can be sure you'll be in a hellhole of a prison for your attack on Inamorata and Deborah." He crouched. "And Elissa." *The woman I love.* "You didn't get revenge on Hawkeye —you sealed your place in hell."

Gun drawn, Johnson arrived and silently took in the situation.

"I want this sonofabitch out of here."

She nodded. "Yes, sir."

Happily he flipped Rollins over again while Johnson wrenched cuffs onto the assailant.

"Emergency medical is en route. Inamorata in the air." Lifeguard's reassuring voice filled the room.

"Send Laurents directly to the main house to take care of Deborah."

"Roger that."

"Get up, you lowlife bastard." With Johnson's assistance, Jacob dragged Rollins to his feet. Then he looked at Johnson. "I don't care what you do with him, but don't let me ever see his face ever again."

"Yes, Commander."

Lifeguard spoke one more time. "Bird is inbound."

Everyone knew where the landing pad was. Things were as under control as they could be. "Walker out." He hit the switch to reset the panic button system, giving them privacy. "Elissa."

Elissa was still in the corner, and he crossed to her then sat next to her. "You did good."

The cat stopped her hissing and dancing and slunk toward them.

"I never believed it was real."

"Let me see your arm." Jacob had to repeat the request before she complied. Fortunately it seemed superficial, but the trauma from the day would last a long time. And for the rest of his life, he'd regret that he'd been away from the house when Rollins showed up.

No doubt she was in shock, and he applied direct pressure to the wound, praying EMTs would arrive soon. "Tell me what happened?"

"I... He forced open the door. I don't know how, since it was locked." Waffle wiggled in close to Elissa, and she absently stroked the cat's head. "The only thing that was close was the teapot. I was behind the door, and I hit him with it. Then I got as far away from him as I could."

She was damn brave. "You sacrificed your afternoon matcha?"

He was happy when she rewarded him with a half smile.

"He tried to come after me."

Even after she'd brained Rollins hard enough to break the ceramic? "So what happened?"

"Waffle."

"Waffle?"

"She attacked him and ended up tripping him."

"In that case, we'll get her all the bacon she ever wants."

"I think she earned it."

Then, seemingly annoyed with the attention, Waffle stood, stretched, then sauntered off.

In the distance, the unmistakable whir from the helo signaled that Hawkeye's A-team had arrived to deal with the authorities and clean up the mess. "I'm so proud of you."

She leaned into him. "I was so scared. Especially... The gun. My ears are still ringing. I think maybe they will be forever."

He didn't bother with platitudes. She'd go on, and she'd get better. The events would fade, but she'd never be entirely the same again. He regretted she'd ever gotten wrapped up with Hawkeye. Her biggest sin was a compassionate heart.

"I guess it's safe to go home now."

"Yeah. But you don't have to. And I'd prefer you never did."

"Jacob..."

Any further conversation was interrupted by a sharp staccato beat on the stairs. Inamorata—no doubt. If she had a first name, no one knew it. But there was a large office pool with bets. Always cool and composed, she was the best fixer he'd ever met.

Without announcing herself, she entered the apartment and glanced around, taking in every detail. "Commander Walker." She nodded.

As usual, her blonde hair was pulled up, and she wore a slim-fitting pencil skirt and stiletto heels. "Medical technician is right behind me."

"Good." The sooner they were here and gone, the better.

She walked across the room and crouched near them.

"Ms. Conroy, I'm Inamorata. Hawkeye speaks highly of you. And with good reason. I saw the feed. If you're ever looking for a job—"

Jacob's protective instincts flared. "You can fuck the hell right off, Inamorata. And take Hawkeye with you. Go do what you're paid to do."

For the briefest fraction of time, he thought she might smile.

Instead she pushed to a standing position and left without another word.

As promised, two emergency technicians strode in, carrying bags. They checked Elissa's vitals and bandaged her up.

"You can take over-the-counter pain reliever if needed."

Since discretion was of utmost importance to Hawkeye, the firm kept an assortment of professionals on call, meaning employees and clients rarely visited a hospital.

"Rest and hydrate, and don't do any more than necessary."

When they were alone, he stroked back her hair. "You ready to get back to the main house? Or we can stay here as long as you want."

"Is Deborah okay?"

"Let's go see." He kept his arm around her as they walked back to his home.

Deborah was still there, and the two women fell into each other's arms and held on tight.

Agent Kayla Fagan took a step toward them, and he held up a hand to wave her off. Fagan nodded and leaned against the counter to wait.

"Agent Fagan was going to take me home, but I couldn't leave until I saw you."

"Me? I'm concerned about you. What happened to your cheek? Are you okay?"

"He hit me when I wouldn't tell him where you were."

"Oh my God." Elissa reached out her hand as if to touch Deborah's face, but then didn't. "I'm so, so sorry."

"Don't be. I'm told I might get a black eye. And it will make a great addition to a Ski Bunny story one day."

Elissa shook her head. "If you don't find an illustrator, let me know. I can never repay you for what you did today."

"You'd have done it for me."

"You were really brave. Thank you." Elissa pressed her palms together. "Did someone go to get Adele?"

If he hadn't already been in love with Elissa, it would have happened at that moment. After all she'd been through, she was concerned for his housekeeper's daughter.

"My sister went to the school." A river of tears washed down Deborah's cheeks. "I was so scared for you."

"No need. Waffle tripped him and took him down."

Deborah wiped her face with the back of her hand. "Are you kidding me?"

"Swear to God." Elissa crossed her heart with her index finger.

"What a good kitty! I always knew she was perfect."

Elissa grinned.

"But what about you? Is your arm okay?"

"This?" Elissa brushed two fingers over the bandage. "It's superficial."

Jacob knew she was lying. From experience, he knew it hurt like hell. "Take some time off," he told Deborah. "As long as you need. A month. Two. You'll get your full paycheck." And a big juicy bonus, even if she opted never to come back. He wouldn't blame her for that.

"I can't." She shook her head. "You need me."

"I'll have Hawkeye send someone until you're ready to come back."

"Do you really mean it?"

"He does." Fagan made the promise as she moved forward. "If you're ready, I'll drive you home. Someone else will bring your car."

Fagan was a skilled professional, and she was easy to talk to. There was no one better to debrief a victim of a horrific experience.

"Maybe I'll finish writing the Ski Bunny story."

"The first Ski Bunny story," Elissa corrected.

They both laughed.

After the two women hugged again, Fagan took control, offering plenty of reassuring words and helping Deborah find her purse before ushering her out the patio door.

No doubt the scene on the front porch was still being secured, and Fagan would do her best to ensure Deborah didn't witness it.

"Can you give me a few minutes?" He filled the kettle and turned it on. "Agent Johnson will stay with you. I want to wrap up a couple of things with Inamorata. Then I'll be back. And I'll be yours as long as you want me."

She nodded and took a seat on a barstool.

He walked to the small circle of people surrounding Inamorata. When she saw him, she nodded, then detached herself from the group.

"Status?"

"Mansfield didn't make it. GSW."

Gunshot wound. "Fuck."

"Appears he leaned past the driver. Had his gun in hand, but not fast enough."

He raked his hand through his hair wishing he'd sent Rollins to hell while he had the chance. "Delivery driver?"

"Deceased."

A total, complete goat fuck. "Need this place cleaned up. And the cat taken care of. Bacon every day."

"Excuse me?"

"You heard me. I'm getting Elissa the hell away from here. I'll file my report later."

"The job is done, Commander."

"It's just started. And it's Jacob."

She smiled. "Good wishes for all your happiness in the future."

"If you're a praying woman, pray she'll have me."

"I'll do that."

A man from the group called out her name. "If you'll excuse me." With a nod, she strode off.

Jacob returned to the house, waved Nan Johnson away with a silent thanks, then slid onto the stool next to Elissa. An untouched cup of Earl Grey sat in front of her. "How about we get out of here for a few days?"

She tilted her head quizzically to one side.

"Are you serious?"

He grabbed his phone and pressed the key on the side. "Hey, Lifeguard. Gonna need reservations for two at a cabin in Steamboat Springs. Plenty of privacy."

"Not my specialty, Commander."

"I'm sure you can find someone who can help."

"Believe I can."

And then he remembered that he'd ordered his truck to be disabled. "And a vehicle. Tell Hawkeye not to be a cheap bastard this time."

"Already have one ordered—for Inamorata."

"I'm sure she won't mind me taking it."

"Roger that."

When he slid his phone onto the countertop, Elissa looked at him. "Steamboat?"

"We need to get away. Rest. Maybe have a bottle of wine. On Hawkeye's tab."

"A nice bottle?"

"Very nice." He nodded. He was ready to have her alone, to confess his love, and pray she didn't turn him down and walk out of his life. "How soon can you be ready?"

CHAPTER TEN

HAWKEYE

"This is luxurious." Elissa turned a slow circle.

Jacob hadn't just procured a cabin—this was a high-end house, no doubt for world's elite who traveled to Steamboat to ski.

"I hope you're pleased."

As he'd promised, a nice bottle of wine—bubbly, even—was chilling in a silver ice bucket. Nearby was a charcuterie board and plenty of fresh fruits. It was more a honeymoon than an impromptu escape.

"Shall I pour you a glass?"

"Yes. Please." *Or just uncork the bottle and pass it over.*

The afternoon had been surreal. From the attacker, to being injured, to watching the Hawkeye Security team in action.

She'd had no idea what she'd been swept up in.

After she video chatted with her parents to prove she was okay, Elissa and Jacob had left the ranch. For most of the drive, she'd been quiet, hardly noticing the scenery as she replayed every single event of the day, and the biggest thing for her was the fear that she might never see Jacob or her parents again. Determinedly she'd refused to allow that to happen. Though she wasn't a fighter, she summoned the strength that had helped her to leave her ex and the determination that helped her deal with her dad's cancer, and she'd channeled them into determination to fight back.

After opening the champagne, a label even Jacob said he recognized, he looked across at her. "Are you doing okay?"

"I am now."

"Now?"

"That we're here." *With you.*

Even though it was summer, Jacob had lit the electric fireplace when they arrived. Despite the size of the place, the atmosphere was cozy. And she had his assurances that it was safe.

The threat was over. Rationally she knew that, but it would take time for life to return to normal.

Jacob had allowed her to listen in to all of his conversation with the Hawkeye team. Rollins had hired hackers to get the information he needed, and the FBI was now working the case. From what Inamorata had learned, Rollins had two of his employees observing the ranch. They knew what time deliveries were made, and noted the frequency of the drone passing overhead. The attack on Mansfield had occurred within sixty seconds of his last-ever radio check-in.

He brought her drink to her. "You really did a phenomenal job, Elissa. I'm damn proud of you."

"Really?" She accepted the glass.

"Yeah. Really."

They tapped the rims of their glasses together.

"Look, I know my timing sucks, but relationships aren't my strong suit—"

"You're ready for me to leave." Despite what he'd said over the past few days, in her heart, she knew it would end. Unusual circumstances had thrown them together, and it had upended both of their lives. Having some sort of affair had been predictable.

But just as predictable, they had separate lives. He was a man of the land, and she had a full life in the city with her parents.

"What?" He dragged his free hand through his hair. "Jesus, Elissa. What the fuck? No. How could you think that?"

Dumbfounded, she stared at him.

"It's the opposite. Entirely." He put down his glass, untouched. "I started to fall in love with you the first night we scened, when you offered your trust. I didn't recognize it at first. But this afternoon—" He broke off and looked away.

"Love?"

When he met her gaze again, his face was haunted. "I was scared as fuck that I wouldn't make it back in time. And I didn't know how I'd live without you. I've found peace with you, in bed, in the way we laugh together. Nothing gives me more joy than your happiness. And then... You asked Deborah about Adele."

Gently, oh so very gently, he captured her shoulders, taking care with her injury.

"For the first time in my life, I'm thinking about a future, about passing the ranch on to future generations. You're the only woman I've ever wanted as a wife."

Unable to fathom his meaning, scared that she was misunderstanding, she remained silent.

"I'm messing this up. Elissa Conroy, I want you to marry me. To spend our lives together. To be the mother of our children."

Everything he said was making her wildest dreams come true. Then he dropped to one knee, completing the fantasy.

"Will you say yes?" He captured her hand. "Tell me you love me and that you'll be mine, Elissa." His voice held an entreaty. "Will you make me the happiest man in the world?

Will you allow me to spend every day trying to make you happy?"

"Jacob, I..." Everything they'd gone through was pushed aside. All that mattered was this moment. "Yes. I love you. Being married to you is my dream. I can't imagine anything more perfect. I want to be your wife. I want us to have kids."

He grinned. "Four?"

Her heart was racing, and she was giddy from excitement. "No. Two."

"To start."

"I thought you were kidding about having that many." Frantically she shook her head.

"Having babies with you is not something I joke about. We can get started whenever you want. I'll let you set the pace in case you need time to recover."

Her mouth fell open when he stood and plucked her glass from her hand. He placed the delicate flute on the mantel before sweeping her into his arms and turning toward the stairs.

"Hold on to me, Elissa."

For the rest of her life. "Always." She grabbed his shirt for stability. "This is getting to be a habit I like."

"I've got a few more habits I'd like to establish with you, Ms. Conroy."

"Do you indeed, Mr. Walker?" She snuggled against the strength of his chest. "Would you like to talk about them?"

"I do believe I'd rather show you."

"In that case, Sir..." She gave him her cheekiest grin. "What are you waiting for?"

When they reached the master bedroom, he carried her inside, kicked the door closed, then proceeded to show her exactly how he intended to keep her happy for the rest of her life.

For the first time since they'd been together, Elissa was up before Jacob. She turned over in the bed of their borrowed home and watched him sleep.

Yesterday, when he'd stormed into the garage apartment, tension and fury had channeled deep lines beside his eyes. Afterward, when he sat next to her on the floor, he'd offered a reassuring smile, but concern for her had darkened his green eyes.

Last night, their lovemaking had been incredible, but he'd been gentler than she wanted. When she asked for a scene, he said she'd gone through an ordeal and he wanted her wound to heal first.

The only thing she'd wanted was to forget the horrible fear when that man, Rollins, crashed through the door and the terror that rocked when she was afraid she might never see Jacob again.

If she'd had any doubts about her love and devotion to him, they'd vanished in that moment. She was committed to spending forever with him, no matter the sacrifices.

Sometime around two, Jacob had dragged her against him and muttered soothing words until she responded by turning over and blinking her eyes open. Screams from her nightmare had awakened him.

For an hour they'd sat up, and he listened while she talked about the experience she'd been through. He hadn't dismissed anything she said, and instead reassured her that processing it would help her move beyond it faster.

Comforted, she'd drifted off in the security of his arms.

This morning, in the soft, filtered light of dawn, he looked a decade younger. Gently she smoothed back a lock of his dark hair before sliding from beneath the covers and silently walking to the closet to find a pair of jeans and a T-shirt. Then she slipped into the plaid shirt he'd lent her when they took a moonlit stroll after dinner.

In the kitchen, she found a jar containing an assortment of teas, and she selected a calming one. Today, she didn't need caffeine.

And since he always took such good care of her, she made a pot of coffee for him before going out onto the deck to enjoy the new day, and the first one of their future together.

She'd just taken the first sip from her cup when he joined her, the waistband of his jeans seductively hanging open, his denim shirt unbuttoned to reveal the lean lines of his abs and the sleeves turned back to show off his biceps. "I don't think there's a better-looking man on the planet."

"No?" Holding an oversize mug, he took a seat across from her. "Then we have something in common. I don't think there's a more beautiful woman in the universe."

Elissa angled her head. "It seems we're charter members of our very own fan club."

"Membership does have its advantages."

"Such as."

His grin was wolfish. "Exclusive access to other members."

"I'm interested in hearing more about that."

"Oh. You will. Without a doubt." He took a drink, then skimmed his gaze down her body. "How are you feeling today?"

"A million times better. Physically as well as emotionally."

"I'm glad to hear that."

"Thank you for letting me sort through it last night."

"In every way, Liss, I will be here for you."

The nickname was new, intimate. No one else had ever called her that, and she smiled at him, liking it.

"After your bath, I'll change your bandage. And we can go into town for brunch, maybe do some shopping."

"If it looks as if it's healing, can we do something else with our day?"

"Hmm." He stared into his mug, pretending to ponder her meaning. "Like what?"

His perplexed expression was so comical she had to laugh. "I want to have my wicked way with you. Reverse cowgirl so you can spank my ass while we have sex."

He arched his eyebrows. "That was specific."

"And even if my arm is hurting, we can still manage that."

"I'll be the judge of that."

"Come on, it has to be better than lugging shopping bags around for me. Right?"

"Woman, at what point will you realize I won't compromise your health? I'll carry a thousand bags before I let that wound get infected." He placed his cup down, clanging it onto the metal table. "The reverse cowgirl while I slap your sexy little butt will definitely happen. When I say."

She scowled.

"Give up the fight. I'm the Dominant."

"And you have my permission to say so." Her words were carefully selected, provocative and cheeky.

He grinned then, something more feral than playful, and her stomach took a nosedive. "Okay, subbie. Off your ass and up the stairs. I'll have a look at your injury and then decide what kind of punishment is in order."

His words thrilled her too much to even pretend to apologize.

He was the man she wanted, the Dominant she needed. No manipulation. No games. Nothing but love and understanding.

"I have one question, Liss."

She gulped. "Sir?"

"Why are you still sitting there?"

Immediately, happier than she'd ever been, she pushed back from the table. "Just on my way inside, Sir."

"The faster the better."

Laughing, she raced across the living room and dashed up the stairs, with him close behind her.

When he reached the bedroom, he slammed the door, then stripped her before backing her onto the bed and spread her legs wide, devouring her with his masterful tongue even as he slipped his fingers inside her.

If this was a glimpse of what awaited her, she never wanted it to end...

EPILOGUE

HAWKEYE

"I can't believe this is happening."

Jacob grinned at his beautiful bride-to-be as their driver eased to the curb in front of the Gallery Royale in New Orleans's French Quarter for Elissa's first-ever opening. Immediately cars started honking, and a bicyclist darted around them.

"I'll be standing by, Mr. Walker. With tonight's traffic, give me a few minutes' heads-up."

"Thank you." After exiting the car, Jacob rounded the hood to offer his hand to Elissa. She stepped out in strappy high-heeled sandals and a formfitting red cocktail dress, alluringly cinched at her waist with a sparkling silver belt. A stylist had done her hair, scooping some of it up and allowing a few long, curly tendrils to tease the sides of her face. Her scent was that of success with an undertone of sweet vanilla. To complete the look, she'd added red lipstick, and the shade had to be Tempting Torment. It took all of his restraint not to suggest that they get back in the vehicle and return to their suite at the Maison Sterling. As it was, he had to be content with the knowledge that she'd be beneath him, surrendering, within a few hours.

Earlier in the day, they'd met Claire Richardson, the gallery's owner, and walked around to double-check that everything was hung the way Elissa wanted and that the placards were with the correct piece.

And now, the gallery was closed to the public. Fairy lights danced around the windows, and music from a live jazz band beckoned.

A tuxedoed woman opened the door for them. "Good evening, Ms. Conroy. Mr. Walker."

Once they were inside, Elissa leaned in closer. "Am I supposed to pretend I'm not awestruck?"

He laughed. "You'll do fine." He plucked two glasses of champagne from the tray of a passing server. After giving her one, he raised his drink to her. "You deserve every moment."

"You made it happen."

"I had nothing to do with it. The talent is yours. And you got the paintings together to do it." She'd worked her ass off, day and night, to make it happen, and he did his best to be the supportive man she needed in her life. When she forgot to eat, he took food over to her. And he welcomed her to bed when she finally joined him each night.

After their time in Steamboat Springs, they'd taken a trip to Denver so he could meet her parents, and she could inform them of her decision to marry him.

Mr. and Mrs. Conroy had shocked Elissa into silence by announcing they were selling the pub. They no longer wanted to work so hard, and their time in Ireland had shown them they wanted to travel while they still had the energy.

Elissa had been nervous that she would be letting her parents down by moving away, but they reassured her that they had no plans to stay in Denver. In fact, they were planning to sell the business to Joseph.

Then her mother had said they may want to purchase a cabin in Steamboat so they could be near Elissa when she finally decided to have children.

Though Patrick had sipped a whiskey and leaned back to stay out of the conversation, Ann had agreed that four children would be perfect.

Seeing Elissa happy made Jacob's life complete. Well, almost.

There was the little detail of getting her down the aisle. She wore his engagement ring, and they'd decided to start trying to have a baby after the opening. Which gave him some ideas for the upcoming evening when they returned to their suite. All he had to do was control his ravenous hunger for a few more hours.

Her portraits were hung in the far end, past the final arch. The room was constructed with half-round faux art deco pillars attached to the walls, creating secondary framing for the paintings.

He understood why Julien Bonds had selected this gallery. It was elegant, high-end, and most definitely catered to a clientele with eclectic tastes. "Shall we?" He offered his arm.

"Look at me. All confident and everything."

Accepting her invitation, he swept his hungry gaze over her. Excitement radiated from her. "Most definitely confident."

"Right." She nodded. "Confident. I belong here."

He laughed. "You wouldn't be here if you didn't."

"Right. Right again."

The back door was open to a private patio, and that was where the band was playing. A full-service bar was set up near them.

The gallery was large, and the lighting was perfect to bring out the deep, rich colors of her oils.

"I can do this."

"There's no doubt."

They mingled for a few minutes with the crowd that was larger than expected. One woman raved about how much she loved *Waiting for Him*, and Jacob went to greet a Hawkeye trainer—Torin Carter. The man had met his wife on a mission in the Crescent City and had fond memories of the Big Easy. When Hawkeye mentioned he intended to don a suit and attend the opening, Torin had opted to join him.

"I'm thinking of buying one for Mira. I think it would be a perfect present to give her when the baby's born. One of the subjects bears a resemblance to her."

"Excellent choice. I'm sure she'll love it." He glanced over at Elissa to be sure she was okay. He'd stayed nearby in case she needed him, but far enough away that she could talk to the invited guests. And as he expected, being in the spotlight made her shine.

The gallery owner walked over to Elissa to shake her hand, and Elissa beckoned Jacob to join them. He immediately excused himself to stand next to her while Torin searched out an assistant to complete his purchase.

"Congratulations. We've already sold one of your paintings."

Elissa's mouth parted. "I… I don't know what to say. You mean a print, right?"

"No. An original. *His Pleasure.*"

"Oh my God, that's amazing. Surreal. I'm not dreaming, am I? Should I pinch myself?"

He couldn't be prouder. At Bonds's urging, she'd priced her paintings considerably higher than she was comfortable with. "I think you've just sold another." He nodded toward Torin, and Elissa clasped the heart-shaped pendant Jacob'd recently bought for her.

"You're certainly one of the hottest artists around right now, Ms. Conroy. And I'll do a formal welcome and introduce you in a few minutes, if that's comfortable for you? We're waiting for a couple more guests."

Including Hawkeye. And maybe Bonds would grace them with an appearance.

"Of course." Elissa nodded. "That's totally fine."

With a nod, Claire moved on to speak to other people.

Elissa was going to say something, but before she could, a woman approached, holding her handwritten invitation to the event. "Do you mind autographing this for me, Ms. Conroy?"

She blinked but recovered the instant the woman offered a pen. "I'd be happy to."

He accepted the champagne flute she asked him to hold. It seemed Elissa was stepping into the shoes of stardom as if they had been custom fit for her.

After returning the stemware to a server, he wandered outside and got caught up on the latest Hawkeye cases with Torin. Jacob was glad for the time—it reaffirmed he didn't miss the job one bit.

About thirty minutes later, the music trailed off, and Claire asked for everyone's attention. She gave rave reviews about Elissa's talent and suggested she was someone to watch. "You know how you all wish you'd have bought Bonds stock when it was under a thousand dollars a share? You know how you promised yourself you wouldn't ever miss an opportunity like that again? Well, tonight is your chance. By tomorrow, with all the press coverage and reviews, Elissa will be a household name, and if you want to add a Conroy to your collection before you need to take a second mortgage to pay for it, this is your one and only chance."

As if for reassurance, Elissa reached for her pendant and touched it, but instead of pausing, she continued to raise her hand, and she gave a friendly wave.

A lightbulb flashed as a photographer captured the moment forever.

"Do you mind saying a few words, Ms. Conroy?"

Elissa smiled. "Thank you for being here, and I hope to have the chance to talk to every one of you personally." Her words sounded natural even though she'd practiced at least a dozen times. "I appreciate the way you've reacted to the pieces of my heart and soul that you see on the canvas. Every painting has meaning, and I'm grateful to share it with you."

Of course, the first picture she'd ever finished, *His*, was on the mantel in their dungeon, in the room he'd built for her. Of course he hadn't known it at the time, but he'd created the space with the idea of having a cherished submissive, and he wanted a private place for them to explore all the nuances of that type of relationship. He'd had no idea how multifaceted their dynamic would be or that it would change, evolve, become even more meaningful.

The first night he took her into the room, they had a conversation about the rings he'd attached to the floor. She'd mentioned being chained to them while they were in front of a fire, with him sipping whiskey while a gentle snow drifted down. She'd trusted him enough to do that.

He'd shared a fantasy of his own—her being on all fours, secured by a collar around her beautiful neck, having no escape as he slid a plug inside her ass, then took her pussy from behind.

He'd watched her press her hand to her heart as he talked, and he'd sworn to show no mercy. And he hadn't.

And his beautiful Elissa—his beautiful submissive—had begged for more. Last week, she'd even brought a collar to him while he was working on his accounting program. She'd knelt at his side, looking up at him, and asked him to fasten it in place.

He could never have asked for anyone more perfect for him.

"I'd also like to acknowledge my future husband, Jacob. Without him, I would have never met the deadline for this showing."

Jacob bowed to her.

"And to a good friend..." She glanced in Hawkeye's direction but didn't call out his name. "Thank you for setting all of this in motion."

He and Torin both looked toward the corner. Jacob hadn't been aware his friend had even entered. Like everyone else, he was wearing a tux, and no doubt he'd walk away tonight with a few more clients. There was no better place than New Orleans to meet people who needed to protect their secrets.

"To Julien Bonds, connoisseur of everything significant—"

People looked around for the Genius, but he wasn't in the room.

"Thank you for the wonderful equipment that I use when I'm creating." More photos were snapped.

"And most of all, I'd like to thank Claire Richardson and the entire staff at Gallery Royale for your belief in me and for hosting this exquisite event."

The guests applauded, the music struck up again, and the waitstaff moved into motion with canapés and other appetizers.

Elissa returned to his side and slid her palm against his. He was leaning over to kiss her when Claire swooped in. "I'm stealing her away. I have a social media influencer who wants to meet her."

He had no idea what that was. "I assume that's a good thing?"

Claire ignored him and beckoned to a young woman with bright pink hair.

At a loose end, he sought out Hawkeye.

"I'm glad to see Elissa happy."

"She's happy you came."

"Hell, after what Bonds said—kinky shit—" Hawkeye smiled. "I wouldn't have missed it. Looks like she's quite a success."

"Two of her portraits have already sold."

"I'm sure it will be more by the end of the night. Claire has a great eye for up-and-coming talent. And her opinion matters. When she tells people to buy, they listen."

Right then, the lights flashed.

"Pardon the interruption..." A bigger-than-life-size holographic image of Julien Bonds appeared in the middle of the room.

A gasp rocked the air as patrons automatically stepped back to make room for the tech rock star. The music abruptly ceased, and silence echoed off the walls.

"He likes to make an entrance."

Jacob looked at Hawkeye. "He does indeed."

Though his image was comprised of a million shimmering parts, Bonds was both a presence and an enigma. He wore a white collared shirt, a thin bright-yellow tie, a gray jacket, blue jeans, and horrifyingly garish hot-pink shoes with glowing green laces. When he moved, the Bonds logo on his athletic shoes lit up.

"Where are you, Elissa?"

"Uhm..." Even as Claire nudged her forward, Elissa looked around for Jacob.

More than half the gathered attendees whipped out their cell phones for pictures and videos. Since Bonds was a notoriously private person, banning cameras when he attended events, this was a once-in-a-lifetime occurrence.

Elissa found Jacob's gaze and shrugged. He grinned and gave her a thumbs-up. With his gesture, Bonds had ensured she'd be catapulted to the upper levels of the art world.

She neared the hologram and stopped.

"Ah. There you are." He waved his hand through the air. "It's the hour, and you are the woman of it."

"I… Am I?" She shook her head and laughed. "What I meant to say is thank you for being here."

"From the moment I saw your kinky shit—"

"Snooped through my hard drive is what I think you mean."

Go, Elissa. Jacob grinned.

"Well." Bonds cleared his throat. "Hmm. Well, then. The data had been delivered into my possession at the time, and it was a simple procedure of transferring it to your machine that is totally safe from any prying eyes."

Hawkeye cleared his throat as he'd been the one to authorize said transfer.

"At any rate, I needed to have something for my personal collection. Which is your most expensive offering?"

"Forever." Claire supplied the answer, pointing toward the gilt-framed portrait occupying prime space on an oversize easel. It was as if she'd been prepared for the moment.

And maybe she had been.

"It's a hundred and twenty thousand dollars."

Bonds staggered back a step.

Eyes wide with shock, Elissa spun to face Claire, who was grinning beatifically.

"I'm sure we must have a bad connection." At Bonds's absurd comment, people laughed. The transmission was flawless. "Did you say…" The leader of the first company in history to be valued at a trillion dollars took a breath, as if unable to comprehend that figure, wringing drama from the moment. "One hundred thousand dollars?"

"No." All eyes were on Claire who was clearly playing her hand well. "I believe I said a hundred and fifty thousand dollars."

Jacob wouldn't have missed this moment for anything.

"Does that include shipping and handling?"

Claire arched an eyebrow. "Are you haggling, Mr. Bonds?"

"Well, a dollar is a dollar."

"Not only does it not include shipping or taxes—it doesn't include my handling fee."

Elissa looked back and forth between the two, and Jacob wasn't sure he'd ever seen a paid production that was this compelling.

Bonds grinned. "A bargain at thrice the price. I'll arrange for shipping—and handling—myself. Elissa, a pleasure meeting you. I look forward to adding more of your creations to my curation." With that misspeak—intentional or not, no one ever knew—Bonds vanished with sparkling fanfare.

Stunned, silent reverie hung in the air before everyone began speaking at once.

One of the assistants draped a purple SOLD sash around the painting.

Jacob said his goodbyes to Hawkeye and sought out Elissa. She appeared shell-shocked, and he leaned down to whisper in her ear. "You've arrived."

"Over a hundred thousand dollars?"

"I'm glad I got in when I did." Though she hadn't wanted to take money from him, he insisted that a deal was a deal. And now, in a matter of months, his investment had soared in value. Not that he'd ever part with it. To him, it was priceless.

The band resumed playing, this time at a louder volume that continued to feed the electric buzz that Bonds had sparked.

Champagne flowed freely, Claire spoke to the woman who'd requested Elissa's autograph, and the gallery's assistants moved about the space with their Bonds tablets, quickly writing orders and taking payments.

"This whole experience has been crazy."

He lifted her hand and kissed it. "And well deserved."

"Since I met you, all my wildest dreams have come true."

"All of them?"

"Well..." Seductively she bit her lower lip before placing her hands on his shoulders and rising onto her tiptoes to create intimacy. "Maybe not all of them."

Hunger and desire flooded him. "Shall we get to work on them?"

"How soon do you think we can escape?"

He glanced around the room. "You've got a legion of fans hoping for a moment of your time."

"Okay." She nodded. "An hour?"

"Meet me in the courtyard. There's a gate we can use. I'll have the car waiting back there."

"One hour?" She checked her watch, then brushed a kiss across his lips. "Don't be late. We have babies to make..." She paused and straightened his lapels. "Sir."

"We have...?" For the first time ever, she'd made him tongue-tied.

She smiled. "If you're ready, so am I."

"Are you sure? I know we talked about waiting until your opening, but I didn't know you meant it immediately after."

"I've never been more sure of anything."

Love and lust collided, forcing a rush of primal need through him. He needed to possess her, be in her. Holding that passion momentarily in check, he held her, cherished her, and pressed a gentle kiss to the top of her head.

"So we're agreed, you'll be on time?"

He was considering summoning the car right this moment. "My Liss. You can bet everything I own on it."

"Good. I can't wait to have your children."

Grinning stupidly, he watched her sashay back into the crowd. He couldn't wait, either. Months ago, he'd been alone, a broken shell of a person, and now... Now? Her love had breathed air into his life.

He'd do anything, everything to make her happy.

Even though she was talking to a young couple, she looked over her shoulder to find him. She blew him a kiss and mouthed "Soon."

For him, it wasn't soon enough.

He waited fifty minutes, which was all he could tolerate, then called the driver. Then when she was alone, he strode across the room, swept her up and over his shoulder.

She squealed as the air rushed out of her lungs. "Jacob!"

"Tell me to stop acting like a Neanderthal, and I will."

"No way." She grabbed his tuxedo jacket. "When I talked to you about making babies, I suspected you'd do something like this."

The stunned crowd parted for them as he strode through the courtyard.

In the car, he told the driver to put up the privacy screen; then he captured her mouth in a hungry, demanding kiss. It was enough—barely enough—to sustain him for the few minutes it would take for them to reach the hotel and ride the elevator to their suite.

"Is this how it's going to be, Sir?"

"Oh yes. From this day forward."

"Promise?"

"Yeah." He tugged her head back so she could see the pure honesty in his eyes. "I promise."

She leaned forward, and he took her mouth again, sealing his vow forever.

◊◊◊◊◊

Thank you for reading Hold On To Me. I hope you loved Jacob and the love he found for Elissa. (And don't forget Waffle—who was inspired by my daughter's cat, Tinkerbell!) Hawkeye and his agents have a very special place in my heart. For the men of Hawkeye, the line of duty between bodyguard and client isn't meant to be crossed.

If you like two sexy, dominant alpha males, a steamy touch of BDSM, some great suspense, and a heart-wrenching second chance at love, Come to Me is the story for you. There's a cool million dollar bounty on the head of Hawkeye commander Wolf Stone. Nate and Kayla will do anything to protect him, but will the cost to their hearts destroy them....?

DISCOVER COME TO ME

Spend time with your next unforgettable Hawkeye agent in Trust In Me, a forbidden relationship romance. Inamorata is his boss. His client is the boss's little sister, and her life is in danger. Trace Romero will do anything to protect her. But who will keep the sweet and lovely Aimee safe from his searing need for her?

★★★★★ "...Sexual tension, passion, heat, danger.....love and the inevitable HEA!" *Niki's Book Addiction*

DISCOVER TRUST IN ME

Turn the page for an exciting excerpt from COME TO ME

COME TO ME
CHAPTER ONE EXCERPT

Shit.

Nate Davidson opened his eyes and tried to shake away the stars that had exploded in his head and stolen his vision. It took several tries before the image of strong, tall, dark, and dangerous Wolf Stone blinked into focus. And when it did, Nate was certain he'd never seen anything better.

It'd been a long time. Too damn long.

"You're lucky I didn't tear your fool head off."

Nate flexed his jaw to make sure it still worked. "Feels to me like you did."

"What the fuck are you doing here?" Stone's voice was deep and ragged, cut glass on velvet.

"You're not glad to see me? I thought you'd start looking for a fattened calf." Nate knew what real danger was. It had nothing to do with his battered body or the nasty storm snarling its way over the Rocky Mountains. Danger was Wolf Stone. And Nate was in the bigger, stronger man's sights.

Nate struggled to get his elbows behind him. Damn mountains were made of rock, not the best pillow under any circumstances. Downright painful when you'd had your clock cleaned by a tank of a man. "Mind if I sit up?"

"Stay where you are."

Lying on the ground, looking well over six feet up into Stone's cold blue eyes left Nate at a disadvantage—or, rather, at a greater disadvantage than he usually was around Stone. "Hospitable as always, aren't you, boss?"

"All trespassers get the same treatment."

No matter how hard either of them tried to pretend otherwise, they both knew Nate was no ordinary trespasser.

And Stone was no ordinary property owner.

He'd commanded several missions that Nate had been assigned to. Every person selected had to meet rigorous physical standards. By any measure, Nate was a good-size man, an inch over six feet, two hundred seven pounds of lean muscle.

Still, Stone had him by two inches and at least twenty pounds. Even now, recouping from injuries, Stone had effortlessly brought Nate down. Well, that was an understatement. Stone had tossed Nate like an old magazine.

"Still waiting for an answer to my question, Davidson."

Sometimes, only the truth would do. "When you refused protection, Hawkeye sent me."

"You're here," Stone demanded incredulously, "to protect *me*?" He raised a dark eyebrow in a way that made grown men cower. Nate had seen it happen, and he refused to admit to himself that it made him cower as well.

"Who'd have imagined?" *Ludicrous.*

Stone sheathed his knife. The weapon was overkill. He only needed his hands in order to tear a strip out of someone's hide.

"Tell Hawkeye I said thanks, but no thanks. You can find your own way off the ranch." Stone turned.

If he hadn't been looking for it, Nate might not have

noticed Stone's slight limp. *Stubborn man.* The threat against his life was real and imminent. He was the only eyewitness to the hit that had taken out Elliott and Lisa Mulgrew. Word on the street was that some lucky bastard would get a cool million dollars if Stone didn't make it to court to testify against Michael Huffman, the murderer.

While Stone was holed up in his fortress, he was safe enough. But once he left Cold Creek Ranch, he'd need the backup.

"So," Nate called out when Stone got about ten paces away, "you're not interested in knowing how I breached the perimeter?"

"You got exactly nowhere before your ass was mine." He continued on without looking back.

"Storm's brewing, man!"

"You'll get wet."

Well, hell. Nate collapsed back onto the unforgiving ground. That'd gone well.

Stone disappeared over a ridge, vanishing into thick Ponderosa pines.

In a nearby tree, a hairy woodpecker—nasty little bastard—beat out a staccato that matched the throbbing headache in Nate's temples.

Under any circumstances, he deferred to Stone. The man exuded a palpable loyalty-inspiring authority. Even now, when Stone didn't want assistance, didn't want to be protected, Nate had no intention of leaving. Stone was as determined as the mountains were rugged. Then again, so was Nate.

Hawkeye hadn't recruited Nate for this job. He, plus the helicopter pilot and copilot, had volunteered. It had taken days of planning, and he refused to admit failure.

Half a dozen raindrops pelted his cheeks.

Even in the past few minutes, the storm had gathered

clouds and whipped them together with wind to descend the eastern slope of the Continental Divide.

Could this get any worse?

Lightning slashed through the swollen gray sky, igniting a path of cloud-to-cloud strikes.

Yeah. It had gotten worse.

Wolf Stone, no matter how drop-dead gorgeous he was, was out of his freaking mind. And an asshole to boot. "You left Nate out there?" Kayla Fagan demanded. "Have you seen the weather?"

"He's not made of sugar."

"Meaning he won't melt?"

"Exactly."

"If this is how you treat your fellow operatives, what do you do to your enemies?"

He shrugged. "None of them left alive to tell." He smiled, and it did nothing to soften his features. The quick curve was more wicked than anything, making his eyes darken, reminding her of those few moments of twilight before the sky devoured the sun.

He strode from the kitchen, and she followed. "Mr. Stone—"

"Wolf, or just Stone." He didn't slow down. "And I'm not worried about how I'll sleep tonight." He crouched in front of the hearth, tossing kindling into the empty fireplace grate.

When she first heard he was holing up in a log house on a ranch, she'd pictured a remote, barely inhabitable two-room cabin.

She couldn't have been more wrong.

Wolf Stone enjoyed luxury, and his home was the intersection of comfort and high-tech. This room, more than any other, gave a nod to his heritage. A rug, painstakingly woven by his grandmother, hung from one of the walls. Another rug, not crafted by his family, dominated the area near the fireplace.

In other rooms, he flicked a switch to ignite the gas fireplaces, but in this one, he obviously preferred to build it himself.

Even though she was stunned by his bad behavior, she couldn't help her fascination as she watched him. His shoulders were impossibly broad. Long black hair, as wild as he was, was cinched back with a thin strip of leather. And Lord, he had the hottest ass she'd ever seen, and a cock with plenty of potential.

Not that she'd actually seen it full-length.

But at night, when he thought she was asleep, he walked around the house in the buff.

Last night, his dick had been partially erect, and the darkened view had inspired her dreams and nearly made her forget her job.

Lucky for her, at least part of the time, she was required to have her hands on him. She just hadn't quite figured out how to professionally get him to take off all his clothes to touch his naked body.

Thunder cracked, and she worried about Nate. "I think you should at least invite him in until the storm passes." Even though it was summer, weather could be extreme at this elevation.

"You going to nag me?"

"Convince you to change your mind, using my excellent powers of verbal persuasion."

"Save your breath. Hawkeye doesn't need to squander its resources on me."

Hawkeye Security. The company they all worked for was named after the man who'd founded it, a man she, and most others, had never met. Wolf, she'd heard, was one of his closest advisors.

With their highly trained men and women, Hawkeye provided world-renowned protection. They recruited former Special Forces operators, ex-cops, bodyguards, lots of IT people, and other brainiacs, including some who worked remotely out of small, private offices. The higher the stakes, the likelier it was that Hawkeye would be the firm of choice.

Her teammates were the best in the world. She was proud to be one of them. "Hawkeye brought me in as well," she reminded him. "Maybe he would go to these extraordinary lengths for any one of us, but maybe he wouldn't. All I can say is he obviously considers you important."

Stone struck a match, filling the room with the sharpness of sulfur. "My mind is made up."

"But—"

"I told Hawkeye not to send anyone. I meant it."

"You can have a heart, just until the weather clears. Then you can go back to your regularly scheduled..." She stopped short of saying assholeishness. "Grumpiness."

His mouth was set, brooking no argument. "Let it be."

Huge splatters of rain hit the floor-to-ceiling windowpanes.

Wolf might be able to sleep at night if he left his comrade out there, but she would toss and turn with worry.

Decision made, Kayla crossed to the hallway closet, pulled open the gigantic golden oak doors, and took out a raincoat. She also grabbed her gun and checked it before tucking it into her waistband. She snatched up a pair of compact binoculars and a compass and was shoving her arms in the sleeves of the yellow slicker as she walked through the great room on the way to the back door.

"What do you think you're doing?"

"Exactly what you said. I'm saving my breath." Kayla spared him a glance. "I decided not to argue with you."

"Stop right there."

He spoke softly, but his voice snapped with whiplash force. Despite herself, she froze. She'd faced untold danger, but this man, unarmed, unnerved her. A funny little knot formed in the pit of her stomach.

Kindling crackled as fire gnawed its edges.

"Turn around." His voice was terrifying in its quietness. "Look at me, Fagan."

Struggling not to show the way she was trembling, she turned.

He stood. "I will be very clear, Ms. Fagan. You are here at my pleasure." He took a single step toward her. "I will not be disobeyed."

His statement was loaded with threat.

Wildly she thought of the room in the basement, the one with crops and paddles hanging from the walls. The one she'd been forbidden to enter, and the door she'd opened the first time he'd left the house.

She locked her knees so she didn't waver. "I've never been much for obedience."

"Nathaniel Davidson is far from helpless."

"He's a fellow member of Hawkeye. I'm not allowed to leave him out there. And I won't." She met his gaze and ignored the fury blazing there. "Really, Mr. Stone, I don't care if it gets me fired." *Or worse.* She pivoted and walked away.

The wind whipped at the door, nearly snatching it from her hand.

She turned up the collar of her ineffective raincoat. There was never anything friendly about a Rocky Mountain storm.

She'd grown up in Tucson where torrential rains were common during the monsoon season. They cooled the weather to bearable seventy-degree temperatures, but this—it was freaking like winter.

Fortunately, she didn't have far to trudge. From her conversations with headquarters, she had a pretty good idea of where the insertion was supposed to happen. And in less than fifteen minutes, the ground beneath her sizzling with electrical ferociousness, she saw a streak of orange.

She grinned.

Members of her team were smart. Nate had donned a reflective safety vest. That would, at least, stop friendly fire.

"Davidson!" When she got no response, she called out a second time.

He started toward her. "Come to rescue me, have you?" he shouted above the roar of the wind. "Bet Stone told you to come."

"He sends his regards and invites you to sit next to the fire while he pours you a cognac."

Nate laughed. "How much trouble are you in for coming after me?"

"He didn't threaten to flay the skin from my hide."

"Doesn't mean he won't."

"Thanks. That's a comforting thought."

"He doesn't know?"

"Who I am? No." She shook her head. "He thinks Hawkeye sent him a physical therapist."

Nate grinned. "Do you know enough about that to do no harm, doc?"

"Uh... I watched a special on the internet."

Thunder crashed.

"I ought to write both of you up."

Wolf. Her breath threatened to choke her. How much had he overheard? It shouldn't have surprised her that he'd followed, that he'd effortlessly covered the same ground she had in far less time. The man was in shape, and he kept himself sharp, the same way he had when he led American troops in the Middle East.

Over the lash of the summer storm, his voice laden with command, he said, "Both of you, back to the house."

The wind snatched a few strands of hair and whipped them against cheekbones that could have been sculptured from granite. His jaw was set in an uncompromising line. Out here, in the unforgiving elements, he appeared even more formidable than he had in the house.

Nate glanced at her. "Maybe I will get a cognac after all."

"No fucking chance," Stone fired back.

Cheerfully, as if he couldn't have been happier, Nate whistled and gamely started down the mountainside. No one should be happy about this kind of reception.

"Move it, Fagan," Stone instructed, leaning forward so he could issue his command directly into her ear.

"Yes, sir."

"Did you say something?"

She blinked innocently.

His arched brow told her he hadn't bought it.

Steps short but sure, she followed Nate, leaving Stone to bring up the rear.

Minutes later, the mean-looking sky unleashed a torrent. Earth became mud. Rocks became as slick as ice.

She lost her balance, and Stone was there, wrapping an arm around her waist, pulling her up and back, flush against the solidness of his body.

The sensation zinging through her was from him, not the streak of lightning. "I'm good. Fine."

He held her for a couple of seconds, his warm breath fanning across her ear. What would happen if she leaned back for just a bit longer and allowed herself to be protected in his strong arms? To feel his cock against her? To surrender to the fantasies that kept her awake at night and her pussy damp, even now?

And what fantasies they were.

Last night's sight of his semierect dick had driven her mad.

After he returned to his own room, she'd thought of the crops and paddles in his downstairs room. She'd pictured him using them on her while she gasped and strained, and ultimately surrendered to the inevitable. Turned on and needy, she'd pulled up her sleep shirt and parted her labia to find her clit already hardened.

She'd come with a quiet little mew and wanted nothing more than to scream the house down as his cock pounded her.

What was wrong with her? She couldn't afford thoughts like this with any man, particularly one she was sent to protect. Because of the risk inherent in working for Hawkeye Security, many employees were fueled by adrenaline, and affairs were common. But everyone knew the rules. No commitments. No emotions were allowed to get in the way of the job. But the way he held her was an invitation she wanted to accept. "You can let me go. It's you who needs to be careful. Otherwise we'll be spending the next week undoing the damage."

"So speaks my *physical therapist*."

Did he know who she was?

Before she had a chance to reply, he added, "I want you out of the storm."

He released her, and the chill crept under her jacket. This time, being more careful, she followed Nate's path.

The trip up had taken maybe about fifteen minutes. Down took half an hour. And by the time they reached the home's patio with its outdoor kitchen and oversize hot tub, the sky was spitting out pieces of ice in the form of hail.

Very polite country, this.

Minding her manners, she took off her shoes and left them on a rubber mat, then hung the slicker on a peg.

Kayla told herself two lies. First, that she wasn't stalling. Second, that her fingers were shaking because of the cold weather.

Stone unlocked the back door and indicated she should precede both men into the kitchen.

Nate followed her, and then Stone relocked the door behind them.

"You." Stone pointed a finger at Nate. "What the hell were you thinking?"

Nate took a step back for self-preservation.

Both men dripped water and tracked mud. Neither seemed to care. And neither seemed to notice she was even there.

"Hawkeye didn't assign you," Stone surmised.

"No," Nate said.

"Which means you volunteered." The storm hadn't remained outside. It had gathered force around Wolf and its heat threatened to consume them all.

Nate's retreat was brought up short when he backed into the countertop. "So? What of it?"

"You knew I wouldn't invite you here."

Nate shrugged. "You don't want anyone. Because you're a fool."

"A *fool*?"

"For always thinking you can do it alone. And you damn well know it."

The men were a study in contrast. Fair to dark. Alpha to beta.

"Fuck your ego, Stone. There's no place I'd rather be." Nate's tone was flat, as if that explained everything.

Kayla sucked in a breath when Wolf devoured the

distance to pin Nate against the counter. Nowhere to run. Nowhere to hide.

"Wolf," she said, licking her lower lip.

"You." He shot Kayla a frightening glance. "I will deal with you directly."

Her stomach plummeted to her toes. She was watching two magnificent warriors spar, and if she wasn't careful, she'd be collateral damage.

Read more of Come to Me.

ABOUT THE AUTHOR

I invite you to be the very first to know all the news by subscribing to my very special VIP Reader newsletter! You'll find exclusive excerpts, bonus reads, and insider information. https://www.sierracartwright.com/subscribe/

For tons of fun and to meet other awesome people like you, join my Facebook reader group: https://www.facebook.com/groups/SierrasSuperStars And for a current booklist, please visit my website www.sierracartwright.com

International bestselling author Sierra Cartwright was born in England, and she spent her early childhood traipsing through castles and dreaming of happily-ever afters. She was raised in Colorado and now calls Galveston, Texas home. She loves to connect with her readers, so please feel free to drop her a note.

facebook.com/SierraCartwrightOfficial
instagram.com/sierracartwrightauthor
bookbub.com/authors/sierra-cartwright

ALSO BY SIERRA CARTWRIGHT

Hawkeye

Come to Me

Trust in Me

Meant For Me

Hold On To Me

Believe in Me

Titans

Sexiest Billionaire

Billionaire's Matchmaker

Billionaire's Christmas

Determined Billionaire

Scandalous Billionaire

Ruthless Billionaire

Titans Quarter

His to Claim

His to Love

His to Cherish

Standalone

Hard Hand (Part of the Hawkeye world)

Bonds

Crave

Claim

Donovan Dynasty

Bind

Brand

Boss

Mastered

With This Collar

On His Terms

Over The Line

In His Cuffs

For The Sub

In The Den

Printed in Great Britain
by Amazon